THE STEAL

Book one of the Reclaiming America Series

Jack Burch

It is a daunting task to write a first book. No doubt many have begun the process and failed to complete it. This time I made it to the end of what I hope to be another beginning.

Dedications are often lofty and cumbersome. I would like to make mine simple and brief.

To my Savior, without whom I would be nothing, I owe all.

To my wife, who has faithfully borne with me for some seventeen years. Through all the ups and downs in life, she has remained true and steadfast.

To my kids - yes, Grace, the Jeep is yours. And Matthew, I hope your dreams of becoming an NFL player come true.

Jack H. Burch, II
December, 2020

"The only foundation of a free Constitution is pure virtue, and if this cannot be inspired into our people in a greater measure than they have it now, they may change their rulers and the forms of government, but they will not obtain a lasting liberty. They will only exchange tyrants and tyrannies."

John Adams, Philadelphia, June 21, 1776

THE STEAL

1

New York City, 9:00 EST

A warm mist hung in the air as the dark sedan pulled into the concrete structure. The vehicle paused for only a moment as a security guard dressed in black fatigues checked for identification. The barricade arm lifted and the vehicle surged forward. After four turns and 2 levels, the sedan parked in an eerily empty concrete sub-structure. Located below ground the entrance to Smith & Samson lived in the yellow and red glow of two translucent bulbs, bare and cold. The driver stepped out – along with two other bulky men in dark suits – and walked around the vehicle. The two men quickly scanned the parking area and with a nod let the driver know all was clear. When the heavy armor-plated door was opened a white-haired man in his late 80's stepped out.

Roger Caldwell was a fit man – weighing only 175 pounds and standing 6 feet 3 inches tall – who bounced when he walked. Sixty years of working both with and for his family had treated him well. When he was only 30 years old, he left a brief stint as an economics professor at Cambridge University upon the sudden death of his father to take over the banking firm his family had run since the early 1800's. A man who found what worked and then stayed with it, Roger Caldwell still managed to run 3 miles every morning – although he did so now on a treadmill and under the constant watch of a live-in nurse. His lean form took three long steps towards the double doors and walked inside.

The ride to the 34th floor was shorter than he remembered – new elevators had been installed since his last visit nearly 2 years ago and they were both highly efficient and very quiet. With a whisper the door opened and Roger stepped into a brightly lit and warm office, Mozart was quietly playing in the background. Two steps and Roger met the young secretary.

"Good evening, Mr. Caldwell"

"Evening Miss Chase, how are you today?"

"Very well, sir. Thank you for asking. The gentlemen are all here and awaiting your arrival. If you would like I can bring you coffee once you are seated."

"That will not be necessary, Miss Chase. Thank you."

Roger Caldwell opened the solid mahogany door and was greeted by eleven men seated around a large oak table. The table was old – nearly 200 years – and had a unique design burned into the center, a massive winged-lion surrounded by twelve crescent moons halved by thin scimitars. Each man was similar in build to Roger – the shortest among them was six feet tall, the tallest was six feet four inches – and ranged in age from 52 to 88. Roger was the oldest by six years. The man at the head of the table stood and welcomed Roger.

"Good Evening, Mr. Caldwell, we are glad you could join us."

"I was unaware I had a choice in the matter, Stephen."

"There is always a choice, my dear friend."

Stephen Hammond was young – at least to Roger Caldwell he was. At 58 years old Stephen Hammond was the head of a large shipping corporation which ran nearly 100 cargo vessels between Asia and America. At a net worth estimated to be over 100 billion dollars, the shipping magnate ran his company with an iron fist. His family had immigrated to Boston in 1767 and began building ships which were sold to the English Crown. After the American Revolution Hammonds Ship Builders contracted to build the first four naval vessels for the fledgling nation – and made a handsome profit. When the Civil War broke out it was Hammonds Shipping – now operating three shipyards – who convinced Secretary of the Navy Gideon Welles to invest in iron-clad vessels. During the 1940's Hammonds shipping was awarded massive government contracts to build nearly one-third of all the naval vessels which flew the American Flag in WWII. Every single Aircraft Carrier built since 1943 came from a Hammonds Ship-yard.

Stephen Hammonds looked around the room at each man, letting his gaze linger for just a moment to be certain they were all attentive.

"I believe you all know each other – or at least *of each other* – so I will not indulge you with introductions at this time. As you know it has been the goal of this organization to bring the world together under an economics system which shares a common currency and a common banking system. For over two-hundred years the single obstacle to this has been the strength of the American economy. Our fathers believed that during the Great Depression we would be successful – President Roosevelt did exactly as he was instructed and was nearly able to nationalize the banking and production sectors. Of course, when war broke out, we had to put our plans on hold. With the strength of the dollar after WWII it was impossible to bring the American economy to its knees – believe me, we tried. However, with the help of our friends in Congress we have been able to significantly weaken the dollar to a point where it is nearly valueless."

Several men muttered under their breath at this statement and cast an agitated glance at Stephen.

"Gentlemen, you all know what our ultimate goal is. And while I know many of you have lost significant amounts of money, let me assure you that once the plan has reached fruition our organization will virtually control the entire world economy. Our man in the White House has assured me that the economy will not improve. With the government spending nearly three times the amount it takes in it is merely a matter of time before the system fails. And once this happens the only hope for survival America will have is to join the European Union in a common monetary system."

"How do you plan on dealing with the American people when the government announces its plan to unite with the European Union? Do you honestly believe they will sit passively by and watch as their dollar is replaced with the Euro?" a dark-haired man asked.

"Let me assure you, Mr. Williams, that the American people will follow their government blindly, all you have to do is promise them more money. America no longer has the conscience it was founded upon. It is ruled by the almighty dollar and when that dollar becomes worthless the American people will be more than happy to replace it with something that will fill their appetite for cheap goods."

"So, it begins then?"

Stephen Hammonds looked around the room. With a sigh of relief and happiness he replied, "It has already started."

2

When Roger Caldwell returned home, he went to his office and poured himself a gin and tonic. After two slow sips he walked over to the large flat-panel television mounted to the North wall and turned to MSNBC. He needed to check the numbers and make sure they were headed in the right direction. Unemployment had dipped to 9.8% - the first time it was below 10% in nearly 6 months. The Federal Reserve was considering lowering the Prime rate by .5% - a move Roger knew would only fool the people into thinking the government could actually help them – and consumer spending had dropped 15% this quarter. Perfect he thought. Now if those fools in the Congress would just pass the newest "Stimulation Bill" the economy would begin the slow descent from which he knew it could not recover.

It had taken years to weaken the American economy – the Republicans in power during the late 1940's had refused to increase spending and had actually cut taxes and reduced federal expenditures which resulted in an economic boom that lasted nearly 30 years. When President Johnson signed massive welfare legislation, government spending tripled – and still the production power of the United States continued to expand.

So, they tried to defeat America by supporting Communism, and this too failed. America would never let the world fall to Communism – that was the flaw in the plan. Nobody could defeat America, it was simply too strong, too powerful. The only way the United States could be defeated was to force her to commit suicide. And while it had taken longer than planned, America had slowly been drinking the poison which would bring about her collapse.

Twice since the end of WWII the American system had fallen to its knees – the first under President Carter and the second after 9/11 – but both times the nation shook off the blow and fought back. Now, thanks in part to the economic policies of the Democrats, things were falling perfectly in place. It had been almost too easy – promise the people what you could never give them – Hope and Change, Change and Hope – and they would follow you like blind sheep.   It still amazed Roger how simple the plan was. Elect a man who had no understanding of economics, no experience in running a business and convince Congress that the only way to pull America out of the current recession was to spend more money – to prime the economy exactly as President Roosevelt tried to do in the 1930's. Who cared that FDR's plan failed miserably? Hadn't the history books taught us all that FDR saved America? So far, the government had passed over a trillion dollars in "stimulus spending" and was ready to pass another bill which would raise the debt by more than three trillion dollars. It was too easy; too simplistic. America was on a free-fall towards economic destruction and anybody who happened to get in the way was simply branded a lunatic, a far-right fanatic, or a racist.

Yes, Roger Caldwell could finally relax. His life-long dream was finally coming true - with the collapse of the dollar the only choice for America was indeed to join the European Union. And once that happened his holdings in both Europe and Asia would, by all models he had run, triple if not quadruple. He just had to make sure that none of those crazy "I love America" conservatives popped up anywhere and tried to convince Americans that by returning to the ideals of the Founding Fathers the nation would be saved. But it didn't matter now – the government controlled everything they needed – the military, the production, education, and the media. Soon they would control the entire healthcare system too. No, there was nothing that could stop them this time.

The old man smiled, walked over to the double French Doors leading out to the balcony, opened them and stepped outside. The night was dark and damp. A cold mist settled on the ground and seemed to absorb the shadows. Roger Caldwell was not afraid of the dark, he had been living in it for years.

3

Office of the Speaker of the House, Washington, D.C.

The Speaker of the House was in an ill mood. Already five minutes behind schedule and she still was waiting for the tall man to make his point. The Speaker was nearing 70 years of age – and she felt it. She came from a long line of politicians – her father had been a U.S. Congressman and mayor of Baltimore and her brother had served a term as mayor of the same city. She had moved west after marrying and became involved in politics – the "family business" – after her eldest child graduated high school. Never worried about any opposition – her districts perhaps the safest in the nation – she had been able to promote herself and her personal agenda without fear of voter backlash.

When her assistant told her about the short-notice meeting with the shipping magnate she had at first decided to have a staffer speak with him, but when she was told he was ready to make a significant campaign contribution she changed her mind. But this meeting was going much longer than she was led to believe. She had no patience for people who could not stay on schedule, especially those who were not important. But somewhere one of her staffers – she would definitely find out which one – had penciled in a meeting with this, what was he again? Ah, yes – a ship-builder. She supposed listening to a ship-builder may be beneficial since she was technically the representative from San Francisco, but didn't he realize she was the Speaker of the House? She couldn't waste her time with frivolous small talk. Not with so much to do. But when a man walked into the office with a quarter-million-dollar contribution to your campaign, you made time – after all that is what American Politics was really about now – how much money you could raise. And the people really believed that she cared what they thought – the Speaker of the House cared about two things: her position and her power, and it was money that guaranteed them both.

"...as I was saying Madam Speaker, I really hope that the House can come to an agreement with the Senate on the newest version of the Stimulus package."

"Yes, I do believe that the only way to push America out of this recession is to help out the average working man and woman. My plan would put over two trillion dollars into the economy, creating or saving over three million jobs."

This part of the speech was getting rather annoying even to her. How much longer could they get by on the 'create and save' bit?

"And we can do this all without increasing taxes on those making less than $250,000 a year."

The tall man smiled.

"Yes, I do believe that would work. I am here to suggest that perhaps a somewhat larger amount may be necessary. My corporation could create nearly five thousand jobs over ten years if the demand for manufactured goods increased only ten percent."

"That is an issue we can most definitely discuss in our next committee meeting. I hate to seem like I am cutting this meeting short, but I do have a lunch appointment in the Oval Office. If you would leave your contact information with my secretary, I will be more than happy to schedule another meet, if you would like."

"Yes, Madam Speaker, I understand. Well then, I will most definitely be in touch. And thank you again for taking the time out of your busy schedule."

The Speaker was more than irritated now. She was ten minutes behind schedule and still irritated that that man – how did he ever get elected? – could summon her to his office like she was a common house maid. Her scowl told her staffers to move aside and let her go. As she closed the door to her inner office she looked down at the calendar on her desk and noticed the scribble next to the name of the man she had just spoken with:

Mr. Stephen Hammonds.

The Speaker spent less than five seconds on the man. He would most likely be back to push for more favorable trade regulations or perhaps less regulation on incoming inspections of cargo from China. In any event the Speaker was most impressed with the large donation he had just made. She would let him have five minutes here and there as long as the money kept coming. After all, did she really care about cargo ship inspections? No, she didn't. And whether he was happy or not had no bearing on her re-election. No, she would dismiss this man like the hundreds of other favor-seekers who walked through her office each week. Stephen Hammonds would be no different – just a man looking for some government favor to help him squeeze the American people for a few more dollars.

What the Speaker did not know – could not know – was that her entire future would be changed because of one call the man made. That call would not come for ten more days, but when it did the Speaker would regret ever having met with Mr. Stephen Hammonds.

4

The Oval Office

T he Oval Office is the official office of the President of the United States. Built in 1909 as part of an expansion of the White House by President Taft, the office is built in an oval shape similar in design to the Yellow room which leads directly into the President's bedroom. The Oval Office has four doors: the east door opens to the Rose Garden where the President often holds ceremonies for the signing of major pieces of legislation; the west door leads to a private smaller study and dining room; the northwest door opens onto the main corridor of the West Wing; and the northeast door opens to the office of the president's secretary. Inside the room sits the *Resolute Desk*.

The *Resolute Desk* is a large partner's desk made from timbers of the *HMS Resolute* – a nineteenth century British Arctic Exploration ship – and was given to President Hayes in 1880 by Queen Victoria as a gesture of good will. Few people know that the ship the desk was made from was instrumental in preventing a third war between England and America. The *Resolute Desk* was first brought into the Oval Office by Jackie Kennedy and left only after the Assassination of President Kennedy when

President Johnson allowed it to be part of a travelling exhibition of the Kennedy Library. President Carter returned the desk to the Oval Office in 1977 and every President since has used it.

The President had his feet on the top of the desk and was leaning back in his custom-made chair when the Speaker walked through the secretary's office. In another gesture of the power struggle between the two. the President refused to allow the Speaker to enter through either the Rose Garden entrance or the Western corridor – no photo op's today. If anyone was going to get political credit for the new wave of legislation it was going to be the President – he was sure of that. The Speaker stood on the opposite side of the Oval Office from the President – who glared at her and slowly took his feet off of the desk.

"So, it would seem you have more important things to do today, eh?"

"Spare me the lecture. I was meeting with a campaign contributor – and a large one at that. If you want your agenda pushed through this session you are going to need his money."

"I'm not sure you understand the gravity of the situation here. I'm not asking for your help – I am telling you that this legislation will pass. The Senate is ready to send it to the floor for debate – not that it will matter much – and I am expecting the House to expedite the bill once it reaches committee. This has to move fast and there can't be any hold. You just do what you need to in order for the vote to pass."

"Don't worry about the bill, with our majority we won't even need to debate it. I can call for a floor vote the day it hits and be done with it. The only concern is the amount you are willing to spend. As it stands in the House, we are looking at 2.3 trillion *more* than the last bill – and today I was asked to increase it by even more."

"Well, I think if we go with the 2.3, we will be safe for now. The total amount is not relevant – just so long as it appears we are doing something. The American people won't care one way or the other – just get the dam thing through before the summer break."

5

July 30, 2010, The United States House of Representatives

The House vote went along party lines – 256 to 178. The Speaker smiled as the last name was called and brought her gavel down with a tremendous slam. The vote was officially entered into the Congressional Record and H.R. 256 was sent to the Senate, where the Majority Leader had promised swift passage of the House version. All that had to be done now was to go through the technical formalities of floor debate in the Senate, a vote, and it was off to the President's desk for his signature – another photo-op with 44, not that she didn't have enough pictures with that overzealous community organizer already, but a picture with the President was a picture with the President – she even managed a smile when posing with the previous man to hold the office. That was really a tough one – she could never tell when he'd crack one of those stupid Texas quips and she'd have to laugh and act as if they were the best of friends. That wasn't an issue with the current President – he couldn't tell a Dick and Jane story without a teleprompter, but if a camera was around, they'd all laugh and smile and put on the facade of a happy little family.

As the Speaker gathered up her papers and began

the walk from the House Chamber to her office, one of her staff assistants came quickly up and, in a rather hushed tone, informed her that there was a visitor waiting for her in her office. The gentleman had shown up unannounced and requested a meeting with the Speaker. When told that she would be unavailable for the rest of the day the tall man simply smiled and said he would wait. The staffer, a young brunette from Georgetown University, was unsure of how to handle the situation and did not want to anger either the visitor – who looked rather important – or the Speaker, whose temper was legendary. No, the young brunette simply smiled and turned to find the Speaker leaving the man sitting in one of the plush chairs that decorated the Speaker's Office.

"Do you know what the name of the visitor is? Did you think to ask what he deems so important that he can interrupt my already busy day?"

The staffer was speechless – afraid of that anything she said would either infuriate the Speaker or embarrass her. So, she did what every assistant would do – she hung her head and followed the woman down the hall.

As the Speaker entered her office, she saw the tall man – what was his name – Stephen Hammonds, that's right, never forget a name or a face. She wondered what the gentleman with the deep pockets wanted to discuss this time – and how he was able to make it up to her office on the second floor of the US Capitol Building. Ever since the 9/11 attacks security around the Capitol had become tighter than at any point in the nation's history. It was nearly impossible for anyone who was not a member of Congress to even get past the daily tours which were given out to the public during the day. The Secret Service had agents in every hallway and at every entrance to the building – one could not simply walk in unannounced and sit down in the Speaker's Office without her knowing about it. But Stephen Hammonds had apparently done just that. Who was this man, she wondered again?

"I am sorry to come in unannounced, but I wanted to congratulate you on the passage of this newest stimulus bill. It is quite an achievement on your part."

"Yes, well…thank you."

The speaker was never one to be speechless, but the gaze of this man penetrated her soul like a shaft of light through the darkness and she was paralyzed by fear, intimidation, and excitement.

"My dear Madam Speaker, I trust you will be able to join us in the Rose Garden when the President signs this momentous bill into law. The American people cannot thank you enough for what you are doing for this nation."

"Why, yes…. I do plan on being with the President when he signs the resolution. I was unaware that you would also be there. May I ask what your role in this process has been?"

"I am simply a friend of the American people. Let's say I look out for the interest of those who find the American Economy of great concern."

With that the tall man bowed, turned, and walked away. The Speaker was stunned at how calm and cool the man had spoken. She forgot about her staffer and placed

JACK BURCH

a call to the security office of the Capitol Building. She would find out who this Stephen Hammonds was and exactly how he had managed to waltz into her office in the middle of the day while every member of the House was in session.

"Hello Madam Speaker, how may we help you?"

"Yes, you can start by telling me how someone can just walk into my office without my knowledge or permission. Also, can you please tell me what we have security for if you boys can't see fit to check visitor's with member's offices prior to letting them roam the hallways?"

"I'm sorry ma'am I don't understand what you are referring to."

"I am referring to the gentleman who I just met with in my office. He was there unannounced, without my permission. I want to know who he is and how he came to be sitting in my office!"

"Ma'am, I can assure you that nobody has entered the second-floor area in the last four hours."

"And I can assure you that you are mistaken."

With that the Speaker slammed the phone down and hastily walked out of her office. She was once again late for a meeting, but this time it was with a more liberal leaning cable news program, so she was not overly concerned.

"Wow...that woman is loony, I'm telling ya Roger." John McAteer placed the head set down and turned to his friend and co-worker of twenty years.

22

"What did she say this time? Did the cleaners forget to dust the doorknob again?" Both men chuckled.

"Nah, she claims some guy walked into her office and sat down in her chair without her knowledge. Did you see anyone enter the second floor in the past couple of hours?"

"Nope."

Roger Stillwell leaned back in his chair with a grin on his face. He wasn't quite sure who the tall man had been or exactly what he wanted with the Speaker, but after checking him for any weapons or explosives he had given him access to the Speakers office. And with two kids in college the extra five-thousand dollars he had just made would go a long way.

6

The Chamber of the United States Senate

It is very seldom that the President of the Senate shows up for debates or votes; his main job – that of the Vice President in the United States – seems to keep him fairly busy most of the time. But today was different. The Vice President wanted to be there to witness the passage of what he considered another historic piece of legislation. SR 237 had been hastily written in order to pass quickly. It was essentially a slightly different version of the House Stimulus Bill passed only two days previous.

The goal was for the President to be able to hold a signing ceremony in the Rose Garden on Friday – just in time to hit all the major news networks and give the pundits something to talk about over the weekend. The Vice President would not vote this time – with the Democrats holding 59 seats there was no chance of a tie – but none-the-less he wanted to be the one who officially pronounced the passage. And the President would get a kick out of the fact that the spotlight would be on his administration and not the incompetent Majority Leader. So, it was no surprise when the Vice President entered the chamber and took his place in the high back chair usually occupied by the President Pro Tempore. Few of the men and women in the chamber seemed to even notice his presence.

As the vote commenced the Vice President smiled. The final count was 62 for and 38 against. All 59 Democrats were in favor and two Republicans and one Independent – all from the north-east – voted in favor of the bill. When the clerk read the final tally of votes the Vice President brought his gavel down. A slight applause crept through the chamber as the Senators began to exit. Several of the Republican senators were heading towards the Minority Leader's desk with looks of concern, while most of the Democrats were laughing and patting each other on the backs, confident that they had yet again saved the American people from falling into the great abyss. What they did not know was that the bill they were sending to the President would in fact have just the opposite effect on the American economy – but then again, all that these career politicians cared about was being re-elected. They could not comprehend the vast amount of money they had just authorized the President to spend and therefore could not begin to realize how far their actions would reach.

With the passage of the Economic Stimulus Package of 2010 the United States took one final and fatal step towards economic collapse. The elected officials whose responsibility was to secure the solid foundation of the great American Republic sent their nation into the abyss with cheers and congratulations.

7

P icacho Peak State Park sits within the Sonoran Desert and is located in south-central Pinal County, Arizona, just off of Interstate 10. The park can be reached by taking exit 219 and heading south-west to the park entrance. The park is dry and hot. The most recognizable geological formation in the area is the Picacho Peak – a large slab of ancient lava that rises roughly 1,500 feet above the desert floor. The peak is visible form over thirty miles away and offers panoramic views of the surrounding desert. The average temperature of the Sonoran Desert – in which the Picacho Peak sits – exceeds 100 degrees in the summer and can plummet as low as 40 degrees in the winter.

This area of the Sonoran Desert is one of the wettest in the Southwestern United States receiving between 3 – 16 inches of rain per year, allowing the desert to support a wide range of plant and animal life. The area surrounding the Picacho Peak is full of cacti, herbs, thorny and thornless shrubs. The creosote bush (*Larrea tridentate*) – a ragged looking bush which looks more like the top of a tree cut-off and buried in the sand - is the most common plant, and the saguaro cactus is the largest and the most conspicuous plant in the desert. Many desert animals, such as bighorn sheep, pocket mouse, and pronghorn antelope can be seen roaming the land.

Selma Hernandez awoke wet and sticky with sweat. She felt the steam rise from her already parched skin and the urge for water welled up inside her. She knew that her daily ration of one-quarter gallon would be brought soon by José – the cruel man with the evil eyes who smiled with wicked pleasure every time he looked at Selma. She was the youngest female in the group – younger by twenty years at least – and often attracted the stares of the six men who made sure that she and the other carriers stayed out of trouble.

It had been nearly two months since she had been kidnapped in Mexico City, a somewhat common occurrence she had learned from Rosa, one of the older women who tried to comfort Selma when they were given their daily rest. Selma had been taken to a dark building and was introduced to El Patron – the man who now controlled her, as well as nearly five hundred other carriers. She had learned quickly to not speak and to do as she was instructed. After what seemed an eternity she was moved to a remote complex near the US-Mexico border where she found out that for as long as she behaved, she would be allowed to work for the Juarez Drug Cartel as a carrier taking the product the cartel produced across the American border to sellers in the state of Arizona. This was the fourth trip Selma had been on – and the fourth different route she had taken. The groups changed every time so she realized it was pointless to make friends, even though the older women had tried.

As Selma awoke and rose to her feet she could see in the distance – the sun had not quite set – what looked like a large ragged edge tooth sticking out of the desert. The carriers travelled at night to avoid both federal and local law officials – although the cartel practically owned this part of Arizona. Selma did not know that Arizona had recently passed legislation which cracked down on illegal immigration – SB 1070 – and gave local law officials broad powers in questioning and detaining suspected illegal immigrants. This was of little concern to her – she had given up any hope of escape, and the two men she had seen trying to get away were both cut down by automatic rifles the watchers carried with them.

Selma picked up her pack, strapped it to her back, and waited for the call to move on. As she took one last look around, she saw the strange mountain in the distance. It stood as a reminder that the world continued to go on regardless of her – and she wondered how many other hopeless mules the peak had seen marching across the desert?

The route slowly moved away from the mountain as the wind began to pick up – perhaps a summer rain storm? They were known for their heavy downfall which seemed to last only a few minutes but left a clean and refreshing smell in the air. As Selma stared blankly at the pack carried by the elderly woman in front of her, she noticed that the line began to move towards the darkened peak in the distance. The level desert floor soon turned into a narrow trail which began to climb up the edge of the mountain. As the line wound around the peak Selma noticed that one side seemed to be a wall of stone – the dark made it difficult to see but she knew it was old and seemed to glow with the heat of a thousand years of desert sunlight – and to her right there was an increasingly steeper drop off.

As she neared what appeared to be the peak, she

heard the order to stop and wait. Ahead she heard the sounds of men talking and then what sounded like ropes being untied and metal clanking together. The woman in front of her whispered that this was the point where the group had to cross a deep crevice in the rock which would take quite some time. Selma sat down and waited for what seemed like hours until she heard the people just ahead of her stand and move. She made her way slowly ahead and as she neared what could only be the light from a large flashlight she was suddenly pulled aside.

The dirty hand of Jose wrapped around her waist. She could smell the crusted sweat and dank odor of a man who had not washed in weeks. His breath was stale and hot. Guttural sounds came from his lips as he pulled her close to him. Fear began to well up inside of her – her breathing became short and fast. She began to yell out but one of his hands quickly covered her mouth.

"Don't cry out – nobody will help you, and nobody can even see. I have been waiting three weeks for this night. I have seen the looks you give me on the trail, I know you want me...your eyes tell me all I need to know."

Jose's hands crept closer up her chest as he began to kiss her face. Selma knew what would follow and she also knew that there would be no help. Thoughts of the old woman Rosa flashed through her mind and pictures of the shabby home beaten by years of dust and heat. How beautiful that place seemed now and how wonderful the hard eyes of Rosa were to her. She could smell the flavors of baking bread and boiling beans, feel the soft breeze of the desert wind. Suddenly she scratched at

Jose's eyes with the furor of a trapped Mexican Wolf. As Jose screamed in pain his arms flung out wildly to Selma and he struck her violently in the head. She felt the blow hard across her face and then the earth moving under her feet. Her mind began to scream out in pain as she felt a series of sudden jolts. Her body automatically curled into the fetal position as she fell.

The last feeling Selma Hernandez remembered was a sharp, searing pain in her head. When she came to rest, she did not know she had just fallen over three hundred feet to the bottom of a small crevice. Nor could she have known that the long line of drug carriers moved north along the small trail – seemingly unaware of her absence. No, all she knew for a fleeting moment was pain – then the darkness overtook her.

8

Ron Jones rode the trail twice a day. His job was to make sure there were no visitors in trouble – dehydrated, lost, injured – and to help them if necessary. He carried with him two gallons of water, a heavy first-aid kit, and a few energy bars. In the ten years he had worked for the Arizona State Park system he had yet to find anything worse than someone with slight dehydration. Most of the people he ran across had wandered just a few yards off the trail and were thirsty more than anything else. After ten years in the Army – four of them in Afghanistan – he had seen far worse than anything he ran across in the Sonoran Desert. His current job was pretty laid back and easy. The illegals that came across the border were mostly south-west of here – the drug smugglers tended to stay in more of a direct line from Mexico to Phoenix because it made their trafficking easier to control.

His daily ride – he had managed to convince his boss that riding a horse would be better than the walking park rangers used to do as this would allow him to cover four times the area as well as carry more water and supplies, not that he would ever need anything except a bottle of water here and there – was just beginning. About ten hours and he would complete the circuit and head home. As he began the ascent up Picacho Peak he noticed small pieces of trash strewn along the path. This was odd as most hikers would either carry small plastic bags with them or simply put used articles in their pockets to deposit back at the office.

Ron slid off his horse – a small appaloosa with brown and cream colors – and started to pick up the trash articles. He noticed that the further up the trail he went the amount of trash increased. He also noticed what seemed to be footprints left by a large number of people. Since it was still early in the morning – and there had been no wind or rain to disturb the ground – he could clearly distinguish at least forty different sets of footprints, all close together and in-line with the path to the top. He had been out here yesterday and had seen only four college kids on a two-hour hike. They had all reported back to the office later in the day and he had watched as they pulled out of the parking lot and headed back to Interstate 10. From the size of the footprints, he guessed that these were smaller in size than the four guys from yesterday – and were most likely all women, or at least mostly women. Ron radioed back to the office and told his supervisor – Rick Gutierrez, a loud robust man who loved to laugh – what he had found.

"You need any help out there, buddy?"

"No. It's probably some prank by one of the local high schools. They did leave a bit of trash, but that's mostly wrappers and empty water bottles. I'll head up to the top and make sure they didn't leave us any painted presents."

"Alrighty then. Let me know of you need any help and I'll get Sandra up there to give ya a hand."

"Will do."

With that Ron led Chisum – he had named the mare after the great cattle-rancher of the late 1800's who had nearly single-handedly tamed the New Mexico frontier and put the southwest on the map – along the trail stopping every five or ten feet to pick up pieces of trash left behind. As he neared the pinnacle, he knew he would have to circle around and come up from the Northern side because he could not cross the ravine on horseback and he did not want to leave his mount. He saw some more trash just near the crevice and walked up to gather the few water bottles together. As he turned to head back down the trail, he noticed some tracks heading away from the others and towards the edge of the peak. These seemed different than the others, almost as if two people had been in a scuffle. He bent down to get a closer look ran his hand through the impressions left behind. As his hands traced the outline of two distinct footprints – one was slightly larger than the other – his eyes wandered in the direction the tracks were leading. Ron's heart skipped a beat as he realized that they both moved near the edge of the ravine – and only the larger of the two seemed to come back from the drop-off. He quickly stood up and radioed Rick.

"Rick, this is Ron, you there?"

"Yeah Buddy, what's up?"

"Not sure. Just looks like a group of about 40 or so people – maybe more – were up here overnight. I followed the tracks up to the Picacho crevice and found what seems to be evidence of some type of scuffle. Two sets lead to the edge and it kind of looks like only one comes back. I'm going to take Chisum around to the North side and pass by the bottom there. I'll let ya know if I find anything down there."

"Ok. I'll get on the horn and let Sandra know. She can bring up some extra water of you need it or some trash bags."

"Ok. It'll probably be an hour or so."

"Roger that. Keep in touch."

As he placed the radio back in his hip he mounted up and turned south. The trail would take him back down the East side of the mountain and then around the bottom to the Northern face. It was still early – only 7:45 – and fairly cool so he wasn't too concerned about the heat yet. He glanced around one last time to see if he had missed any of the trash the unknown visitors had left last night. Seeing nothing but the mysterious tracks he nudged Chisum forward and both rider and horse started down the sloping trial. As Ron neared the base of the mountain, he had an uneasy feeling in his gut, not unlike the one he had that day in Afghanistan when his unit was ambushed in the mountain near the small town of Lamar. He still remembered that day and how the only reason his unit came out with only two casualties was because one of his fellow soldiers was able to hold off a group of fifty insurgents while the rest of the platoon was picked up by the big Sokolsky UH-60 Black Hawk. It was that day that Ron became intimately aware of both fear and courage – and how sometimes the only difference between the two was what you did with it.

Seven years later and he could still remember the

exact moment Philip Stone yelled the order to fall back. The last thing he ever thought he would see of the man were the flames erupting from his M-4 Carbine rifle. But at what seemed like the last moment his Platoon leader emerged from a cloud of smoke and – with a smile on his face – seemed to fly through the air and thorough the massive door of the floating helicopter.

As the group sped away Ron heard two sharp cracks followed by a couple of large explosions. Phillip had set down four of his grenades underneath a piece of fallen tin. When the platoon returned the next day, they found five dead insurgents and what appeared to be several blood-trails leading away from the area. Phillip's trap had worked perfectly. He had placed the grenades – pins pulled – under a sheet of roofing tin and then, after firing several quick bursts from his weapon, ran to the waiting helicopter. The smoke grenade one of the soldiers tossed out during the fire fight hid Philip long enough to enable him to make it back. When one of the insurgents kicked over the tin the four grenades went off nearly simultaneously.

This is what the smile on Philips face had been from – the little treat he left them had worked to perfection. And then here – seven years later and in the middle of an American desert – Ron had that same feeling that something just wasn't right. This time, however, there would be no Philip Stone to save the day.

As Ron reached the bottom of the trail and turned North, he lazily glanced around the base of Picacho Peak. There was no evidence of anyone having been on the grounds last night except the tracks left on the trail. These headed back South into the desert and seemed to go on forever. He continued around the foot of the mountain and turned to head back up to the top along what is usually the downward portion of the trail. As he began his incline, he called back to the office in his radio to report in:

"Hey Rick, you there?"

"Yeah. What's up?" You find anything else?"

"Not yet. It does seem as if there were more people coming through here than I originally thought. The tracks come down the north side and continue in a north-westerly direction, almost as if they are on their way to Phoenix. I would guess maybe 40 or 50 total."

"Alright, I'll give Sam a call over at the county Sheriff's office and have him send a car out. Maybe they can look into it a bit more than we can. I hope it isn't any of those dam drug guys, that'd just ruin the day."

"Yeah, tell me about it. Hey, has Sandra left yet? I could use some extra water for Chisum...he's pushing it a little harder than he is used to out here."

As Ron came to the opposite side of the crevice, he had noticed the lack of trash on the trail. He thought that perhaps what was left on the other side was all there was, but he wanted to make sure so he dismounted his horse and walked over to the edge of the crevice in order to make sure nothing had been thrown down there. As he leaned over to look down between the two walls of the peak, he saw what appeared to be the body of a small adult lying at the bottom covered with dirt and blood.

"Rick! Rick! Get an ambulance out here! There's a body at the bottom of the crevice. I'm going to check it out. Tell Sandra to hurry up and get here."

"Roger that."

Ron hoped back up on Chisum and went as fast as he could down to the bottom of the crevice. The trail was fairly narrow near the top so he had to be careful not to run his mount over the edge. When he arrived at the bottom, he saw Sandra just coming up from the south side of the trail and waved her over. He then grabbed his first aid kit and a bottle of water – just in case. He was pretty sure that whoever it was would be dead – especially if they had been out here all night – but wanted to make sure he could do something for whoever it was if there was any sign of life.

As he bent down to check for breathing, he could feel a weak pulse and noticed the chest barely moving up and down. His first thought was to pick up the body and try to get it back to the office and wait for the ambulance to arrive. However, years in the service had taught him that things weren't always what they appeared to be so he calmly looked over the body to determine if it was safe enough to move. He noticed that the person was a female, small in size and probably in her late twenties or early thirties. Her head had a small laceration running from the right ear, up the sided of the head, and ending somewhere near the top – he wasn't sure since it was hidden in a mass of hair which was covered with dried blood and dirt. The woman's left leg had a compound fracture about two-thirds of the way down. Ron guessed it was the Fibula due to its thin size. He could not know if there were any internal injuries but he was certain that it was more than likely the case. How she had survived the fall was a miracle in itself. The fact that she hadn't bled out last night was another one. But this did not matter right now. He knew that they had to get her back to the office somehow and do it pretty quick.

9

P aul Gonzalez was an old man. He had spent thirty-seven years as a Pinal County Deputy Sheriff and was nearing retirement. Having never aspired to anything but his routine life – his wife worked at the local hospital in the cafeteria and his four children had gone to college and then moved away – he was somewhat irritated when the Sheriff had called upon him to go investigate a possible hiking accident out at the Picacho Peak State Park. Wasn't it just his luck that the body had been found just inside the Pinal county line? The poor bum who fell didn't even have the decency to do it a little further south in Pima County. No matter, from what he had been told whoever the unlucky person was would probably be dead by the time he arrived on scene. Wouldn't that be the ticket? Then he would have to wait for the ambulance, fill out even more paperwork, and make a formal report to the Sheriff – probably even notify the news in Tucson about it. What a way to wreck a perfectly boring day.

As he drove down Interstate 10 Paul noticed an ambulance racing up behind him with lights and sirens on. He was cruising at 65 mph – the posted limit was 70 but he wasn't in a hurry – and in the right-hand lane.

As the ambulance passed him, he hit the switch on his radar gun just for kicks. 97 mph. Paul laughed to himself and wondered what the guys were in such a hurry for. He hadn't heard of any accidents on the road or any fires around – even though there were several every year during the summer, this year had been fairly good with only one big fire, and that was out in the middle of nowhere so the fire department sent out a couple of trucks just to make sure it didn't spread.

As he shook his head, he suddenly thought about the accident at the state park – if the ambulance was headed there in such a hurry that meant that whoever had been involved was still alive and he wanted to be there just in case it had not been an accident after all. Not to mention it was a good opportunity to see what his new Dodge Charger could do. He flicked the switch to activate his siren and lights and fully depressed the gas pedal. As the fuel was fed through the injectors and into the combustion chambers of the massive 5.7-liter Hemi V8, Paul felt the car surge forward as his body was thrown deep into the cushioned seat. Within five seconds he was passing 100 mph. He could feel the power running through his body as the vehicle rocketed down the highway.

Five minutes later he took exit 219 and headed west towards the park's main building complex – the newly built visitor center which holds public restrooms, a gift shop, plus vending machines with energy drinks and snacks, as well as the main office for the park rangers. As he pulled into an open parking space, he saw the ambulance parked diagonally across three spaces with the backside pointed towards the trail signs. It appeared the Emergency Medical Technicians were loading the accident victim into the back so Paul got out of his cruiser and walked over to the three park rangers standing about 10 feet away.

A quick glance at the body being loaded onto the ambulance told him that the person was still alive – there was a small oxygen tank on the side of the stretcher with tubes connected to a mask on the woman's face. Her eyelids were slightly open and her head had been bandaged. He noticed a dark stain on the sheet that covered her just about two-thirds of the way down her left leg. A compound fracture, no doubt. The EMT's finished loading her in, closed the back door – the driver could get up front from the inside – and pulled into the parking area and headed towards the highway. Paul walked over to the rangers and introduced himself.

"Morning. I'm Deputy Paul Gonzalez. Seems like there's been a little excitement here this morning?"

He smiled and offered his hand to the biggest of the three – there were two men and one woman.

"Good morning Deputy Gonzalez, I'm Rick Gutierrez and these are Rangers Ron Jones and Sandra Heyward. How are you?"

"Well, I'm alright, although I guess I wouldn't say that for our friend who just left. You guys have any information on the accident?"

"Not sure if it was an accident, Deputy. The lady was really out of it – she fell about 300 feet – partly down a cliff, but mostly through rocks and bushes. We think she hit her head about half way down on a small outcropping of stone which gave her the head injury, but probably also saved her life because it broke her fall enough so that she seemed to have slid more than fell the rest of the way down. All I could make out from what little she said was that she kept calling for someone named Rosa to keep some man away from her."

"I see. Well, let me get my report book and meet you guys in the office?"

"Sure. Inside and just to the left you'll see the door."

Deputy Paul Gonzalez was mad now. His quiet day was gone. Now he would have to investigate what was turning into an assault – possibly attempted murder – and the only witness was half-dead Hispanic woman who spoke no English. Add to that the fact that the crime scene was at the bottom of a 300-foot crevice in the middle of the Sonoran Desert and the temperature was supposed to climb to 105 degrees. Well, at least he could start out in the Ranger's office – that was air-conditioned, he hoped. As he grabbed his report book and pen, he let out a heavy sigh.

After he left the park he would have to go to the hospital and see if he could interview the woman. That meant a long day. He turned towards the visitor center and thought that maybe this would be a quick investigation – perhaps this woman was an illegal who would not talk. If that was the case, he could just write it up and file it. He hoped and prayed that that's all it was. He didn't want to get caught up in some drawn-out case with only three months until he could retire in peace and quiet. Paul Gonzalez shook his head and laughed. Just his luck he thought. Just his luck.

10

President Woodrow Wilson signed Public Law No 43 – HR 7837 – creating the Federal Reserve Banking System. With one stroke of his pen the President committed the greatest act of nationalization of private wealth the world had ever seen. The Federal Reserve Act – the "short title" of the act itself – created the first national bank in the United States since 1836, when the charter of the Second Bank of the United States lapsed without renewal by Congress. The inability of Congress to renew the charter for the Second Bank of the United States was – perhaps foreshadowing modern American Politics – more of a power struggle between the Whigs and Jacksonian Democrats than an economic issue. It was a question of who would control the monetary power of the United States.

Most Americans believe that President Andrew Jackson refused to sign the bill which would renew the charter for the Second Bank of the United States, however the bill was never sent to the President because Congress believed that Jackson would veto the bill. The truth of the matter lies more in the personal politics of the President himself than in any political power struggle. Jackson – who was supposedly an "anti-establishment"

President, having come from what most believed was a background of low-birth and poverty – actually pulled all of the national funds from the Second Bank and placed it in banks which were owned and operated by his friends and political allies.

What most believe was a political move by Jackson to defeat an overreaching federal government was actually the result of a personal feud between the President and Nicolas Biddle – the President of the Second Bank of the United States. The real reason the charter for the Bank was not renewed was because the new Whig party was unable to get enough of their members elected to achieve a veto-proof majority. Had there been enough members of Congress to override Jackson's threatened veto then the Second Bank of the United States would have had its charter renewed and – most likely – Jackson's bid for a second term would have failed. This is, of course, not what happened. When Jackson's plans to defeat the Second US Bank – or to destroy Nicolas Biddle – succeeded, there was no centralized banking system to control the flow of money from the national government to the public – but it is doubtful that the Founder's wanted there to be one, as the idea of a national bank was a highly disputed issue of debate from the nation's beginning.

What happened instead was a continuously repeating cycle of growth and decline – with a general pattern of sustained growth overall – from the early 1800's until the early 1900's. When President Wilson signed the Federal Reserve Act, he was attempting to help stabilize the flow of money throughout the American economy. What he was actually doing was nationalizing the banking system of the United States and placing it entirely in the control of a very small, very select group of individuals. This group would determine, for good or bad, the value of the dollar, and – in essence – whether the American economy would grow or decline. Through the power of the Federal Reserve this small group of twelve people would control the single most powerful economic system the world has ever known.

According to the Federal Reserve Act of 1913, the Bank is charged with providing for the establishment of Federal Reserve banks, furnishing an elastic currency, affording means of rediscounting commercial paper, establishing a more effective supervision of banking in the United States, and several other miniscule purposes. In essence, the Federal Reserve Bank is given the task of stabilizing the flow of money from the federal government – which actually prints the money – to the twelve district banks, and through these institutions to the several hundred member banks who continuously interact with businesses and individuals within the economy.

The power of the Federal Reserve – the Fed as it had come to be called – is immense. The Chairman of the Fed has the power to raise or lower the Prime Interest Rate – the rate at which member banks borrow money form the government, which in turn will help them set the rate at which a business individual will pay for a loan – as well as determine how much currency is actually flowing through the economy. This is all done with an eye on keeping the economy strong and stable. During times of economic growth, the Prime rate may be raised slightly to prevent growth from taking place too fast – as was the case during the 1920's which led to the Great Depression – and during times of economic stagnation the Prime Rate may be significantly lowered in an attempt to promote growth and prevent a significant recession from occurring.

The one aspect of the economy which the Federal Reserve cannot control is how much money the government actually prints. When an excessive amount of printed money floods the economy the value of the US dollar sharply declines in relation to all other currencies in the world. The effect of this massive flooding of the market with currency has is to drastically lower the purchasing power of the dollar and weaken the ability of businesses to invest and increase production. The most significant effect is upon the American consumer. The ability of individuals and families to meet their basic demands is reduced, their spending power is significantly damaged, and while the amount of money flowing in the economy may have increased the actual value of the dollar will decline rapidly.

This results in inflation, a general decline in the spending of money by nearly all areas of the economy, and will begin a cyclic pattern which would – if unchecked – result in hyperinflation, an occurrence when the value of the dollar would be so miniscule that prices would rise to levels on par with that of 1930's Germany. The price of the most basic necessities would skyrocket – a loaf of bread would cost nearly $100; a gallon of milk would cost so much that producers would save money by dumping their product instead of sending it to market. This would all be caused by a sudden influx of massive amounts of paper money into the economy –which is precisely what the 2010 Federal Stimulus Bill was designed to accomplish.

11

*Headquarters, Bank of America, 100 North
Tryon Street, Charlotte North Carolina*

W hen news of the passage of the 2010 Federal
Stimulus Bill was made public several banks
across the nation took a step back. Most wanted to see
how the bill would affect the already weakened economy and, with literally hundreds of billions of dollars in
investments already shaky, a falling stock market, and a
weak dollar, it was uncertain to those who ran the banking industry how this new bill would help strengthen
the economy. The last stimulus bill had saved the largest
banks from bankruptcy – not to mention fill the pockets
of those men and women who had actually caused the recession – but had little, if any, effect upon the economy as
a whole. In fact, the exact opposite had taken place.

When the Federal government passes stimulation
legislation what happens is actually quite simple. The
US Mint, by directive of the President with the authority of the US Congress, prints more money and releases
it into the economy. This is done through a complex
system of printing and re-allocation of funds from the
United States Mint – which actually prints the money –
to the Federal Reserve, through the twelve partner banks

and the several member banks, and into the economy itself. When the currency actually hits the market there is an immediate effect which includes inflation, a devaluing of the dollar, and often a lack of confidence in the economy itself. With a sudden increase in the amount of money available most banks are not willing to loan as much or to spend as much as they normally would. Neither businesses nor individuals see an increase in their income, however they do see an increase in prices. While the amount of money flowing through the economy has substantially increased, the value of that money has diminished to the point where the overall effect is one of a less valuable currency.

This results in less purchasing power and higher prices. This will then result in less money available to small business and individuals. The net effect upon the economy is that the amount of money flowing through the economy has been diluted and the currency has been made nearly valueless. The only way producers can compensate for the decrease in value is to raise prices. This in turn causes the suppliers to raise prices, and then the market places must also raise prices. The part of the economy which actually pays the price for the decrease in value is the consumer. Now faced with massive inflation – and in some cases what is known as hyper-inflation – the consumer sees a sharp decline in his ability to purchase goods. This process is inevitable and can only be stopped by decreasing the amount of liquid capital flowing in the economy.

If the federal government was to reduce the availability of money then the cycle of recession would most likely stop and the economy would correct itself. However, if one wanted to bring the economy to the breaking point all that would need to be done would be to cause a massive influx of dollars into an economy already weakened, and which had a dollar whose value was in decline. Charles Buckland – a low-level analyst with The Bank of America – was watching CNN when the President signed the Federal Stimulus Act of 2010. He immediately looked up the bill and started skimming the text looking for two things: how much money was being pumped into the economy and where those funds would be coming from. He found the answer to the first on page 479 of the nearly two-thousand-page bill. When he saw that nearly three trillion dollars was being released, he shook his head. He doubted whether anyone on Capitol Hill – or even the President – had read the bill and had any idea what amount of money they were dealing with. But the amount in itself was not what disturbed him the most.

As he continued skimming the bill – a rather long and arduous process considering all the legal jargon in it meant to hide its true purpose from all but the most knowledgeable readers – his mind began to see a picture which caused an alarm to go off inside his head. The funding for the bill was not coming through the normal channels – either borrowing from foreign investors or issuing federal bonds – but rather the government was going to simply print dollars. He saved the document to his flash drive and sat in his chair for several minutes. He wanted to get another opinion on the content of the bill and whether his fears were realistic or just an emotional response to his own personal beliefs. He wanted to speak with someone who understood better than he did how the economy worked. He knew some people who worked for the bank who could probably help him out but they would also try to explain it away in terms that benefitted the bank.

What he needed was an outside opinion, someone who had an intimate understanding of the economy and what impact this bill may or may not have. So, he dialed the number of the only person he knew who could offer him an unbiased opinion in terms that he would understand. He hit the quick-dial number on his personal cell phone and waited for the man on the other end to answer. When he was routed to the voice mail, he left a short message:

"Shawn, this is Charles. I just read over the stimulus bill and I had a couple of questions about the funding. I was wondering if you could look over it? I'm e-mailing you a copy of it in PDF format. I'll give you a call around 8:00 tonight my time. Talk to you then."

With that Charles went back to work, but for the rest of the day his mind kept wandering back to the bill. Every time he thought of the stimulus package, he had a sense of foreboding that some massive storm was brewing – a storm from which nobody would be able to hide; a storm so powerful it would bring the country to its knees. He tried to push the thoughts out of his mind as merely those of an overactive imagination – after all surely the people who advised the President understood the economy much better than he did – but the thoughts remained and kept encroaching on the edge of his mind. Well, he would wait until he spoke with his friend from Colorado before he made any decisions on the bill itself. So, he pushed the bill from his mind and went to work on yet another multi-million-dollar investment portfolio. Perhaps one day his own might reach the million-dollar mark and he could then retire and give his family the life he wanted them to have; but that would be years away.

Years he now doubted he would have.

12

S hawn Reynolds sat in his office a tired man. He had spent 25 years as a Professor of Economics at The University of Colorado. He held a Bachelor's of Science in Mathematics from the University of North Carolina at Chapel Hill and a Master's Degree in Economics and Mathematical Theory from the University of Chicago. After five years as an investment banker, he decided he preferred the slower paced life of the university and returned to school. He spent three years earning his Doctorate in Economics from Stanford University. Upon graduation he was offered a position as a guest lecturer and taught undergrad math and economics courses. He understood that having just received his PhD he would have to work his way up to a position which gave him more flexibility and options for research, however he did not expect the opportunity to come so soon.

After only one year of teaching at Stanford he was made aware of a new program that the University of Colorado was starting. This new program would offer courses in mathematics and economics theory. The participants in the program would earn either a Bachelor's or a Master's degree in Practical Economics and Monetary Theory. Shawn Reynolds' area of expertise would be in studying the effects of governmental monetary policy upon the private sector of the economy. This offered him some unique opportunities in both travel and politics. As part of his responsibilities, he would travel to Washington and attend both lectures and seminars on government and the economy. Here he would meet many of the top economists and politicians and be introduced to the many economic professors who advised the top echelon of Washington politicians.

As Professor Reynolds took off his glasses – after thousands of texts books and articles his eyes had begun to fail him – he closed his eyes and leaned back in his leather chair. With a heavy sigh he let the weight of the long day drain away and leave him. He waited only a moment to indulge in the feeling of calm his daily reverie briefly gave him. His mind wandered to thoughts of his wife – the one person he felt truly comfortable around. With her there were no degrees, no lectures, no books to write or to read, and no stress of constantly producing articles and lectures on a topic most Americans did not understand or simply did not care to understand.

To his wife of thirty years his ideas on the economy were a part of him she simply did not understand. It was not as if she never tried, she would sit for hours listening to him discuss the views of such notable economists as Adam Smith, Thomas Robert Malthus, Karl Marx, and John Maynard Keynes. He would go on for hours discussing the differences between supply-side economics and the need for government intervention. His wife would simply sit quietly and listen, not understanding the majority of what he said. To her the economy was all about earning more than you spent, being able to afford some simple luxuries, and planning for retirement. For her, as for most Americans, the economy was no further away than the checkbook or the paycheck. For Shawn Reynolds the economy was much, much different.

Shawn Reynolds saw the economy as a complex orchestra constantly in motion. Each part, while seemingly small in both size and importance, was a vital piece in the orchestra. If any one of the pieces failed to function properly then the entire symphony would be out of tune. The economy was much the same but with thousands of more parts, which meant thousands of more possibilities for failure. When Shawn closed his eyes, he could see the many intricate parts all in motion at the same time. A company investing in raw materials, another integrating some new technology to improve product quality, yet another part of the grand picture was the government increasing interest rates in an attempt to slow growth and prevent another rapid ascent – which would be followed by an equally rapid decline. He could read the sings of how the economy flowed much like a conductor could read the sheets of music and understand how the music would ebb and flow from piece to piece.

For Professor Reynolds his symphony was just as beautiful and dynamic as Mozart's Symphony No. 41. Shawn could feel the vibrant flowing of goods and precious metals like a conductor could feel the sounds of trombones and violins. He could tell if one small piece was out of tune and what the implications of that would most likely be. This is why Charles Buckland had called him. The young man had remembered how much his college professor made economics seem like a course in classical music – comparing the many different parts of the economy to the different parts of a great symphony.

If there was anyone who Charles Buckland would trust in understanding the impact the new stimulus package would have on the economy, it was Shawn Reynolds.

At precisely 6:00 Central time Shawn Reynolds heard the ringing of his office telephone. After two rings he picked up the headset and spoke in his deep voice to the young man on the other end of the line.

"Hello Charles, it's good to hear from you."

"Professor Reynolds, how have you been?"

"Quite well. Susan keeps me busy with the new addition to the home. We just added a vegetable garden and she is intent on a great first harvest this fall, so I have been put in charge of keeping the critters away. But I somehow don't think you called for a lecture on turnips and green beans."

"No, sir. Did you happen to look at that document I sent you? The new Stimulus Bill that just passed?"

"Not really. I glanced over it. Seemed like the usual big spending that has been coming out of the capitol since the Democrats took over in 2006. It's really not much different than the last one, you know?"

"Well, that's what I wanted to talk to you about. While the structure and funding seem to be relatively mundane, the source of the funding is what I was curious about. If you read the sections on procurement of funds, you will notice – at least from what I read – well, it seems like this time they are just going to print the money. I mean there is no basis for the cash. No bonds, no loans, nothing but empty air."

"Really? I haven't looked that deep into it. It is over two thousand pages you know. It'll take a few days for me to read that far."

"Ok. Well, look into Section VII. That's where I remember the procurement of funding. To be honest, I don't even understand it all, but I thought you might be able to give me a better understanding of it. It just seems odd Professor Reynolds. I have never seen a stimulus bill where you couldn't figure out where we were getting the money. I mean, before we would sell bonds and then we borrowed the farm from China. This time, there is nothing there."

"Hmmm, that would be odd. Like I said, I'll read through it and let you know. I really doubt that the folks who wrote the bill would just decide to print money with no backing from either domestic or international bonds. That could really harm the economy. You'd have to want something bad to happen if you did that. Nah, I don't think they did that. It might just be hidden somewhere else in there. But, like I said, I'll read through it and get back to you in a few days, maybe early next week, ok?"

"Sure thing. You can reach me either here or on my cell. Please give me a call as soon as you find it, would you?"

"Sure will. Listen, don't worry, we may not always agree with what those folks in Washington do, but I'm pretty certain they would never do something like this – it would just be too dangerous. I'll call you in a few days. Take care, Charles."

"You too. And thanks again for the help. I really hope you are right."

"Don't worry, I'm sure I am. Ok? Goodbye old friend."

"Goodbye."

As Shawn Reynolds hung up the phone, he hoped that what his former student had asked him to do would prove to be nothing more than a long search for some misplaced information. He was actually looking forward to proving the young man wrong – to still be the teacher and the master of his domain. Yet for some reason he had a slight feeling of concern and foreboding, as if he were standing on the porch watching the sunset and not knowing if the darkness was the night coming or if it was the coming of a storm. If what Charles believed to be in the bill was true, then what he might be seeing was not a storm on the horizon as much as it would be the end of a long bright day. He thought of what Benjamin Franklin had said at the conclusion of the Constitutional Convention when asked about the sun on George Washington's chair. The old sage had claimed it was a rising sun he saw; if Charles was right, then that sun would not be rising any longer – it would be falling quickly and violently into a deep, dark night.

No, Charles had to be wrong. Nobody in their right mind would fill this economy with valueless dollars – that would be like giving a starving man nothing but empty bags from which to eat. Well, he had a few days to figure it out. Besides, there were rabbits to keep out of the garden for now. Those pesky creatures could show up at night and literally eat every vegetable you had. You'd go to bed with a nice new garden full of promise only to wake up with a ravaged pile of dirt devoid of anything but the droppings left behind. Shawn quietly chuckled to himself. Rabbits. He hoped that the government didn't turn out to be the rabbits.

13

S hawn Reynolds set down his wine glass and noticed that his hand was trembling. He had to stop a moment and calm himself. After nearly six hours of continuous reading, he had finally been able to understand the meat of the new Stimulus Bill. When he discovered that the majority of the projects were run by government agencies and that nearly ninety percent of the jobs created would be federal in nature he had paused and opened a bottle of Chardonnay, not bothering to cool it first. After nearly a quarter of a bottle his head began to hurt, so he popped three aspirin and continued reading.

When he finally found the section of the bill describing where the government would actually be ascertaining the funding, he was not sure whether his sweaty palms were due more to the wine or the reading. What he did know was that on page 1308 in Section XXIV of the Stimulus Bill of 2010 there was a short sentence which made the rest of the bill pale in comparison:

"Funding for this act will be procured through the reproduction of monetary standards in line with current Federal Reserve Notes. These notes are to be produced at a number not to exceed three trillion US dollars in value; the Chairman of the Board of Direct-

ors of the Federal Reserve Bank will have the authority to increase or decrease the number of Notes printed by the United State Mint at his discretion as long as the Chairman:

1. Notifies, in writing, the Secretary of the Treasury of any changes no more than three days prior to or after the actual printing, and

2. Notifies, in writing, both the Chairman and the Ranking member of the Joint Economic Committee no more than three days prior to or after the actual printing"

Shawn was dumbfounded. He had spent over two hours trying to find any section of the bill which would override or negate the funding but found none. As his mind began to spin, he wondered who exactly had written this section? He knew it had to be a staffer since most members of Congress never even read a bill – let alone wrote one. But that was not the point. Here was the most damaging piece of legislation his mind could conceive of. The United States government was preparing to inject into the economy over three trillion dollars of currency – and none of it was worth the paper it would be printed on.

Shawn set his papers down and felt his entire body begin to go numb. He could not believe what he had just discovered – he already knew what the result would be: a sudden surge in spending would result in massive inflation. This would be followed by a massive reduction in fund availability which would be just as sudden. The end result would be immensely high prices for goods with little or no money to purchase those goods. Sellers would have to charge high amounts simply because their costs would skyrocket as a result of the influx of capital.

When the supply of money stops there would be nothing left to purchase goods with and consumption would stagnate.

At some point in time people would realize that they could no longer afford even the basic necessities – food, water, fuel – and would, at least in the cities, most likely begin to riot. He had seen this before in many of the Third World nations when there had been a change in government. In an attempt to placate the people and provide them with goods the new leader would simply print money. The cycle was always the same: prices skyrocket as more cash becomes available; the government stops printing in an effort to lower prices. When sellers realize there is no more money available, they raise their prices even higher in order to get as much of what is left as they possibly can. In every single nation where this happened the result was anarchy or rebellion. And none of the countries escaped without massive bloodshed.

Shawn's heart pounded in his chest. He walked to the kitchen for a glass of water. He needed a break. Surely this could not be happening. This type of mistake was no mistake – whoever had written this bill knew exactly what they were doing and knew exactly what the result would be. Someone was trying to bury America in an economic grave and had been able to manipulate the Congress of the United States into passing its own death sentence.

14

The Oval Office, Friday May 14ᵗʰ, 2010. 8:00 p.m.

T he President was already starting to sweat and the cameras weren't even on yet. He knew it was the make-up he had to wear and he also knew that the make-up would prevent anyone watching from seeing that sweat. Funny, he thought to himself, that the very thing that caused you a problem could also prevent anyone from seeing that problem. At precisely 30 seconds before eight o'clock the little red light above the camera – there was only one from which all the major networks and cable channels would receive their broadcast feed – would glow and tell him that it was almost time to start.

It had been the idea of his chief of staff to give a speech from the oval office. It was the most Presidential place for Americans to see their Commander-in-Chief, and the man elected to the highest political office in the world needed to look Presidential. His approval ratings had been falling steadily over the past several months and had just recently dipped below the forty percent mark. As of the previous Friday his overall job approval rating was at thirty-nine percent. His "likeability rating" – whatever that was – was still near fifty percent, but as he had been so meticulously informed by his chief of staff, Americans may like your smile, but that didn't mean they liked *you*. Here was a great opportunity to yet again use a bad situation for political gain.

Eight o'clock. The words began to scroll across the teleprompter as the President read the prepared speech. He had already edited it three times and rehearsed it earlier in the day. Nobody in the White House wanted there to be any mistakes or any negative inflection of his voice. They all knew that the President likes to over-stress and over pronounce certain words and sounds in order to try and get his point across, however tonight he had to appear in total control and exude both confidence and strength. This time the man behind the *Resolute Desk* would need to do no more than read the teleprompter in a strong and even voice.

15

Pitkin Colorado

R on Stone turned on the television in time to hear the President's speech. He had been told by one of his co-workers earlier in the day that the President would be speaking about the economy and the new Stimulus Bill which had just been signed. The hot topic in the service bay all day had been about the speech. Most guys would jokingly guess how many jobs were saved this month or how many new government jobs were created. Some guys even went as far as to place bets on whether the teleprompter would fail and the President would be left staring into the camera like a deer in the headlights. Ron just wanted to see how President would use the free air time to try to pull even more wool over the eyes of the American people. He had heard that the Stimulus Bill was massive, but he wasn't quite sure what massive meant this time. It seemed to him, and most of the people he knew, that one day massive might mean five-hundred billion dollars and the next day it would mean one-trillion dollars. It wouldn't surprise him one bit if today massive meant two trillion dollars. Well, somebody had to feed those sweat-shop Chinese kids. He just wished it wasn't him.

Ron sat back in his recliner and turned up the volume when he saw the seal of the President of the United States fill the screen. Ten seconds later the face of the President appeared. He noticed that the man was wearing a light blue colored suit with a white shirt and a dark red tie. Pinned to his left lapel was a large American Flag pin – the same kind which he had been lambasted for not wearing during the campaign.

"Well Ron, doesn't he look patriotic?"

"So did Benedict Arnold. Here, listen up, he's starting."

"My fellow Americans, good evening, and thank you for giving me the opportunity to speak to you from this hallowed office. It is always humbling to know that you have given me the great responsibility, honor, and privilege of being the President of this great nation. Tonight, I speak to you not as the leader of the Free World or as the Commander-in-Chief, but rather as a husband and a father. The past few years have seen our economy shaken to its knees but you have remained strong and faithful to America. Together we saw the worst economy since the Great Depression fall upon this great land. We have all been either directly affected by the loss of jobs or we have known a friend or relative who has lost their job. And yet we have remained strong. When you elected me to this office you sent me here to stop the bleeding and fix not the outward effects of years of Washington politics, but to seek out the causes of those failed policies which created the current recession. We have done just that. We have passed legislation which will create millions of new jobs. Working with Congress I have been able to sing legisla-

tion which created over five million new jobs and saved over three million jobs. But there is much we still need to do. The Stimulus Bill I signed in 2009 helped stop the downward spiral of our economy. Millions of Americans were able to keep their homes, their cars, and their jobs.

Now we must begin to rebuild our economy. We must all work together to dig ourselves out of the dust and debris of an economy nearly destroyed by Wall Street greed and wasteful government spending. Throughout our nation's long and illustrious history, it has been the role of the Federal Government to prime the economy – to jump start it when it stalled. President Wilson did this when he signed the Federal Reserve Act in 1913, and FDR again did this during the 1930's when the nation was in the midst of the Great Depression. A Democratically controlled Congress passed stimulus legislation in 2008 which was signed by former President Bush. Over a year ago I was able to push through Congress and sign the American Reinvestment and Recovery Act of 2009 which stopped the fall of our economy.

Just this morning I signed into law the Stimulus Bill of 2010 which will enable our economy to begin the climb back to prosperity and success. I know there are folks out there who will tell you that government spending cannot help. I say to those who do not believe in the American Dream that this new law will strengthen our economy and prevent another recession of this magnitude from taking place in this nation again.

As part of the Stimulus Bill, I just signed the United States Department of the Treasury has been ordered by me to send tax refunds to every American household *making less than two-hundred fifty-thousand dollars a year. Each household will be receiving a refund of two thousand five-hundred dollars for every adult over eighteen years of age. Parents will receive an additional one-thousand five-hundred-dollar refund for every child.*

> *This refund is yours to spend or save any way you like. This is money you have earned through hard work and a spirit that says never quit, never give up. It is time that the government gives back to its citizens that which it has taken and wasted for so many years. I am confident that this will not only jump start our economy, but will also lead to a more financially secure and stable future, not only for ourselves, but also for our children and grand-children.*

> *Thank you again for allowing me to come into your homes and spend a few minutes of your valuable time with your families. Thank you, and May God bless the United States of America."*

Ron Clicked off the television and looked at his wife. A thin smile crept across his face as he stood up and walked into the kitchen for a glass of water. Well, maybe something a little stronger would better fit the moment.

"You want anything?"

"Nope. Just my check,"

"Your check? You mean *our* check, don't you?"

"You heard the man, Ron. Each adult. That means you get a check and I get a check. And since you won't be home when the mail comes, it must mean that I get two checks!"

"Hold on a second! Who said anything about me giving you my money?"

Ron and his wife laughed and sat close to each other on their old couch. It had been a long time since she had seen the sparkle in his eyes, but she was sure it was there now.

"So, what do you want to do with our new fortune?"

"I don't know. Let's see, twenty-five hundred for each of us and fifteen-hundred for each of the kids. What's that? Nine-thousand five-hundred dollars, right?"

"Sounds right, yeah."

"Good. That will be just enough to buy that new boat I saw down at Clements' last week."

As Ron finished his sentence, he felt the soft smack of a couch pillow on the back of his head. His wife began giggling and laughing. Ron picked up the pillow, jumped up and turned to throw it back at her when he felt another blow from another pillow. This time the offending missile had been launched from across the room. As he bent down to pick up the second pillow, he saw his wife disappear down the hallway. Friday night and his kids were at the movies and most likely would not be home for another two or three hours.

It had been a long time since Ron had felt like things might get better, but tonight he thought that maybe, just maybe, they might be turning around. As he chased his wife down the hallway, he could feel his stress and worries falling off of him like the clothes he was throwing on the floor. Tonight, he would leave it all behind him. As he stepped into the bedroom, he saw his wife's beautiful face glowing. He closed the door as she laughingly said "Come here, baby. Let's get an early start on our stimulus spending."

Ron Stone smiled. He could finally see the light at the end of the tunnel.

16

Two Hundred and fifteen miles away Shawn Reynolds turned off his television and stared blankly at the screen. He still couldn't believe what he had just heard. Over the next several months the federal government would slowly be putting over three trillion dollars of liquid capital into the economy. What a stroke of genius, he thought. Not only was the poison coming from the government, it was being administered disguised as tax refunds, money the government owed to the people. He knew how popular it would be among Americans that the government would be sending money to nearly every person in the country. What he knew that virtually nobody else did was that those checks were not tax refunds, they were death certificates. He had to tell someone who could let others know how catastrophic the new "tax refunds" would turn out to be. Someone with enough clout to make a big enough noise that could not be ignored. And he knew exactly who that someone was.

17

When the President of the United States gives a speech from the Oval Office there are usually several people inside of the room at the time the speech is given. The President sits at his desk, one or two of his advisors are standing just off camera, the speechwriter is generally present to make sure the speech is properly given and in case of a malfunction of the teleprompter the speech writer has a hard copy available immediately for the President. The camera crew includes a director, the camera operator and a technician who is in charge of the connections and who relays information from the Oval Office to the media control room. Tonight, was no different, with the exception of one person which nobody seemed to notice.

Rafael Abdullah Aphasia was nearly sixty years old and had very light-colored skin – so much so that when he was growing up in Iran his friends would often make fun of him claiming he had a western mother. Rafael would become enraged by these taunts and more often than not wound up in a fight which he would seem to always lose. It was difficult for the skinny young boy to defend himself from the physical beatings of boys who were both older and stronger than he was, so he found another way to fight them – he would use his mind.

By the time Rafael was twelve years old he had discovered two very important things about himself that would help him achieve an incredible amount of success in life: his light-colored skin allowed him access to more western banks and social circles than most of his countrymen, and his intelligence allowed him to take advantage of those encounters with very powerful people. He had been able to amass a large fortune – which he used to help fund such organizations as Hamas and the Palestinian Liberation Organization. He stayed away from groups like the Taliban or men such as Osama Bin Laden because Rafael understood one thing that these men did not – you could not destroy the Great Satan – which is what nearly every Arab called America, either directly or when the cameras were not rolling – with direct or even indirect violence.

To men like Rafael Abdullah Aphasia the best way to bring America to its knees was to destroy the one thing which made the nation so powerful – the belief that America was different and special among the nations of the world. If one could destroy American's belief that their nation was unique and greater than all others, he would destroy the nation – with no foundation upon which to stand the country would crumble in upon itself, and the people of Allah – the true believers – would be able to simply walk right in and takeover.

He had started nearly thirty years before – with the building of over fifty mosques throughout the country. It was his idea to bring the Koran to the prisons – this would kill two birds with one stone. His imams could convert the most dangerous members of society to Islam and train them to hate America – all under the guise of teaching peace and repentance. How often Rafael would laugh to himself knowing that the Americans were helping him – indeed often paying him – to spread the cancer which would eventually kill them. Only in America could a religion designed to promote the subjugation of others be actively promoted among the deadliest members of society all in the name of preparing those members for acceptance in mainstream America. In his home land of Iran men who murdered, raped, or sexually abused children would be given a trial and then summarily executed by either the firing squad or the more ancient method of public stoning. In America they actually believed that you could change the minds of such demented individuals and prepare them to be – what was that the Congressman had told him, oh yes – to be "active and contributing members of society." Well, Rafael would indeed make them active and contributing members of society, although he doubted whether the kind of activity, he had in mind was the same as that ragged old man from Massachusetts.

Today, however, Rafael was present in the Oval Office for a much different reason. He had met the President over twenty years ago at a fundraiser for one of the poorer Chicago neighborhoods. The two had discussed ways to bring more community involvement into the area and try to end the rise of crime and drug usage – especially among the teenagers who wandered the streets at night. After the fundraiser Rafael invited the young man with political aspirations to his home – or one of the many he had in America – to discuss his political future. It was during this meeting that Rafael realized that he and the man who now sat in the Oval Office had a great deal in common.

As Rafael began to inquire into the background of this young politician, he would uncover truths that, if his plan were to become reality, would have to be hidden to such a degree that if any person were to even try to uncover the truth that individual would need to meet a sudden and violent end. Rafael had pledged to the young community organizer the backing of the Muslim-American community and all the money that came with it. He would be the silent partner who could guarantee a quick rise to political prestige and power. When the young man first ran for public office, it was Rafael's friends who were able to present the media with rather damaging information on the young politician's opponent. This information was so negative that the rival was forced to withdraw from the election. Rafael's young firebrand won his first election with no opposition.

As the years went on this good-looking and vibrant speaker would win seats in the Illinois House and Senate. When Rafael believed the time was right to move his plan forward, he urged the young politician to seek the office of United States Senator. While the idea of being a Senator was appealing, several members of the organization wondered if they were not moving too quickly. Rafael assured them that the time was ripe for America to elect a man to the office of the President who did not fit the historical mold of a wealthy white male. The first step in this process was to win an election to a national office.

The US Senate was the most obvious choice as this would allow them six years to move forward to the next level of the plan. Some had suggested beginning with the House of Representatives, but Rafael had made it very clear that if they had to win an election every two years it would be even more difficult to succeed with their ultimate goal of winning the White House. For Rafael Abdullah Aphasia the ultimate goal was to place the right man in the office of the President, thus giving the organization unfettered access to the inner workings of the American political and economic systems. This would essentially allow them to control the economy of America as well as the national political agenda. With the proper man in the White House Rafael could not only influence the domestic and international agenda of America, he could virtually change the course of history through the power and influence of the Office of the President of the United States.

Today Rafael was in the room simply as an invited guest while the President gave his speech. He wanted to witness first-hand the words which would put his plan in motion. As soon as the President finished and the camera was turned off Rafael placed a call on his Blackberry to the head of his organization in order to assure him that the plan was indeed moving forward as they wanted. As the President of the United States wiped the make-up from his face and drank a half glass of ice water Rafael Abdullah Aphasia hit the send button on his telephone and waited for the man who had masterminded the entire plan to answer. Fifteen seconds later Rafael heard the smooth melodic voice of Stephen Hammonds.

"He has finished the speech."

"Good. Now we need only to wait for the Treasury Department to begin the printing of the checks. At that point it will be nearly impossible for anyone to stop us."

18

Selma Hernandez awoke in a small hospital room. She could feel pain in her leg and head, but she could only see a haze. She tried to move and found her body strapped into the bed she was in. As her mind began to clear she could feel the pain increasing. She felt a constant throbbing in her head and a series of deep, sharp pangs surging through her left leg. She had no idea what had happened after Jose had pushed her – she could only remember thinking of the old lady and hoping she would see her again.

"You have been hurt very badly," a gray-haired woman said, "and you are very lucky to still be alive."

Selma understood every word. She knew the woman was speaking in her native language of Spanish and her face quickly filled with fear. Her eyes grew wide and her heart began to race. She knew that if she was in a hospital, she could easily be found by the man called El Patron. It would only be a matter of time before she was either back carrying illegal drugs or she would be made an example of. She had heard of others who had tried to escape and none of them ever returned alive. Some had been murdered in sight of the others, while a few of the escapees would be found days later cut up and dumped in a city fountain as a warning to those who crossed the cartels.

"You need to remain calm. There is nobody here who will harm you. What is your name?"

"Selma." Her voice was scratchy and dry. But it was her voice, she knew.

"Selma, such a beautiful name. My name is Juanita. I am the nurse assigned to your care during the day. You took a nasty fall down at Picacho Peak. You received a nice gash in your forehead and your lower left leg was severely broken in the fall. The doctors had to put six pins in it in order to straighten you out."

Rosa just stared at the elder nurse. She was still full of fear that at any moment the Patron and his hired hands would burst through the door and take her away. She could not stop her mind from imagining all that would be in store for her. As her heart began to beat even faster, the elderly nurse smiled and reached towards a device attached to the bed. Rosa noticed there were two bags hanging from a metal hook which had tubes leading to her right arm. She could still not move.

Rosa began to cry as she saw the nurse press a little dark button on the machine – she was sure that whatever was being done would only make her life worse and full of more pain. As the drugs began to take effect she thought again of the old woman and wondered why she ever left. She could feel her body falling into a slumber and could do nothing as her mind fell away to emptiness. The last thing she remembered before the darkness came again was the face of the old woman smiling down on her.

19

R on Jones was on the phone when Paul walked through the office door. He motioned for the deputy to have seat and quickly finished his call.

"Sure. Ok. Well, the deputy just arrived so I need to go. I'll call you later. Bye."

"So, how's the young girl? Did you get a name yet?"

"Oh, I guess she is in and out of it. They got her drugged up pretty good, leg's in a cast with some pins in it. Only person who has talked with her has been a nurse or two. Said her name is Selma, Rosa. I don't know. Either her name is Selma and she wants to see someone named Rosa, or it's the other way around. Either way I'm pretty sure she isn't here legally."

"Yeah. Well, maybe she doesn't even know where here is?"

"I suppose that might be it, but you know how these folks are. Just going to be another one coming here making us pay for their medical bills. I wouldn't doubt if the girl is half way pregnant by now. Then there'll be some more little anchor babies for your tax dollars to care for."

"Well, I doubt she is pregnant, and even if she were pregnant, well the fall alone would probably have killed the baby. Anyway, I'm sure you didn't come here to discuss the economics of illegal immigration, did you?"

"Ah, no. Well, let's see. You sated before that you saw a trail from what looked like several people hiking up on the peak and when you went down around to the other side you found this woman? Correct?"

"Yes, sir. She was pretty bad off. I thought she was pretty much dead, but as you know she was alive, although not by much."

"Ok. Well, do you have an estimate of about how many people you think might have been up there? Maybe based upon how many tracks you saw?"

"Maybe thirty? I'm not sure. I'm pretty sure that there were more than twenty mostly because I picked up about thirty empty water bottles. But if I had to give a guess, I would put the number between thirty and forty."

"Ok. Why would you say that many?"

"Well, for starters the number of empty bottles. Most groups of people who go up there take all of their trash with them, but every so often someone leaves something behind. This time however, it was the opposite. Seems like everyone left something. The fact that we never saw them kind of makes be believe they were here between eleven and maybe three in the morning? The last person out of here usually closes the door around six or just after. I was out on horseback until around five-thirty and saw no signs of anyone coming from the south."

Paul thought for a moment.

"So, they most likely didn't even get in the park until a couple of hours later. And they were gone by the time we found the woman. That was about seven in the morning and her blood was dry, so she had to have been out here for at least a couple of hours. There were no signs of anyone looking north, if they had only been there an hour or so you probably could have seen them from the road when you left here, so I'm thinking they had been gone for at least three or four hours."

"I see. And you found no other signs of trespassing except the empty bottles?"

"There were some wrappers from some kind of energy bars. The writing was in Spanish, so I couldn't tell you exactly what they were. They were put in the trash with everything else though."

"Ah, yes. Destroy the evidence, always a good idea. Ok then. Well, thanks for your time. I'm pretty sure that's all I will be needing from you guys here, so I'll just be heading back. Let me know if you think of anything else."

"Oh, do you know which room she is in? I thought I would stop by and see how she is doing."

"Um, let me see," Paul rummaged through his pocket until he found the card with the room number on it, "yes, here it is. Room 312, Phoenix Baptist Hospital. You might want to call ahead though and give the nurse a head's up. The girl is on some heavy meds and it's just as likely she'll be out of as not."

"Ok, thanks. Well, have a good day deputy."

"Yeah, you too."

Ron thought of calling the hospital to check on the young lady but thought it would be better to go see her. Since he was the person who found her, he felt compelled to at least check up on her. He would go as soon as he finished his paperwork. That would give him the time to drive up and stay for a while.

20

Shawn Reynolds arrived at Reagan National Airport at 8:43 p.m. on a Tuesday evening. His flight was fairly routine with the exception of a little turbulence as they crested the Appalachian Mountains. He was always amazed at the differences between the Rocky Mountains and the older, much smoother Appalachians. It was like travelling back in time a million years. While the Rocky Mountains were higher and more awe-inspiring, Shawn thought the Appalachians were more like an old friend welcoming you back to the place you grew up in. In a sense that was exactly what he was doing.

As he left the airplane and exited the loading bridge – he had brought only one carry-on bag which held three days' worth of clothes and necessities – he saw the old man standing off to the side. Shawn stopped for just a moment and gave the man a quizzical look.

"John, how did you get up here? I thought they only let ticket holders past the counter now?"

"Oh, I guess it comes with age. One of the security guards is the husband of our department secretary and when I told her I was coming to meet an old friend she asked if I would like to surprise you at the terminal. One call and – poof! Here I am."

The old man gave Shawn that caught-with-your-hand-in-the-cookie-jar look that had endeared him to so many students – Shawn was one of them – for nearly fifty years. As the two began the slow walk to the waiting car Shawn began to fill the man in on the reason for his visit.

"I brought the paperwork, well it is on a flash drive, so that you can look it over. I wanted to be here in person so we could discuss some of the more intricate details of the bill."

"Ah yes. Well, I took the liberty of looking over the bill myself. You know, one of the benefits of being so old is that I can get those pesky graduate students to do my work for me when I want," the old man chuckled softly, "and with two Doctoral candidates working for me it is almost like I am already retired. All I had to do was mention that I would like to look at this bill and what do you know? The next morning, I had two copies of it bound and waiting in my box. I think next time I might mention I want to read Adam Smith in German – just to see what happens."

The two shared a laugh and stepped out in to the humid evening. The old professor, who had been a mentor to Shawn on many occasions, drove them to his home just across the Potomac River from Washington, DC. The old man lived in a century old home on Nash Street in Arlington Virginia. He had chosen the location because it was within walking distance to the US Marine Corps Memorial. The professor's father had been a Marine captain during the Second World War who had died at the Battle of Iwo Jima. The old man would often walk around the memorial thinking of the father he had never met, but who loomed large in his mind. His mother had remarried after the War, but she had always made sure that the professor knew the sacrifice his father had given – a sacrifice he often believed many Americans today would be unwilling to give.

As the car pulled into the driveway and Professor Reynolds opened the door he was immediately struck by the heat and humidity. He could easily understand why most Americans believed that the capitol city was built on a swamp, even though that was untrue.

Most people who visit the nation's capital are awed by the buildings and the history, but few realize that before it was home to the most powerful people in the world it was made up of farmland and tree covered hills. The location for the capitol was part of the Compromise of 1790 – a shrewd political agreement between Alexander Hamilton, James Madison, and Thomas Jefferson – which resulted in a southern location for the capital. In return for placing the city in the south several southern congressmen voted in favor of Hamilton's plan for the national government to assume the debt carried by several states as a result of the American Revolution. The exact location for the new capitol was actually chosen by George Washington – who had spent several years as a surveyor prior to his political and military career. President Washington chose a parcel of land located along the Potomac River which originally included land on both the northern and southern banks, however the land originally ceded by Virginia was returned by Congress on July 9th 1846 in part because the recession of the land would give the state of Virginia two more representatives in the Federal Congress.

The two men walked into the home and sat down in the old man's office. The professor offered Shawn some coffee and a pastry. As the two began to sip the hot beverage the old man began the conversation.

"Well, I have been looking over the papers you sent me and I must say that on the surface the bill seems to be a good deal for America. Most people would see it no different than what FDR tried to do during the Great Depression, you know? Prime the economy and get it going."

"True," replied Shawn, "but most people don't know that nearly everything that FDR did actually made the economy worse."

"Well, I know that, and you know that, but when did politicians start worrying about what old college professors know? All they would do is find some economic 'expert' to refute you and – well, there goes your reputation, eh?"

"Yeah, well."

Shawn did not know what to say. He knew his old mentor was right in what he said. Whenever anyone had disagreed with a President in the past fifty years there would be a slew of so-called "experts" who would give some speech or meet with some Congressional committee and claim that whatever the President said was true was indeed true.

Most Americans failed to realize was that over the past fifty or sixty years the national government had been following a series of economic policies which were specifically designed to both weaken the dollar and cause as many people as possible to be reliant upon the Federal Government for their subsistence. This is known as the Cloward-Piven theory of economics.

In this economic strategy several groups – namely anti-government organizations, militant anti-poverty groups, and violent civil rights organizations, would work together with the poor of America to create a political crisis. The violent nature of the protests would force the government to re-think the social and economic structure of the nation. In the end, the result would be a massive redistribution of wealth from the upper and middle class to the poor. The national government would guarantee such things as assistance with rent, food, child care, and medical care. In essence the United States would be transformed from a capitalist society to a socialist society through federal regulation of the economy. This is what Shawn Reynolds believed the Economic Stimulus Act of 2010 was trying to accomplish.

"Well, you know that when the government starts printing all this money and dumps it into the economy prices will skyrocket."

"Yes, that is just elementary economics. But as long as there is some type of backing or some kind of basis for the funds, I think we will be ok. We may see inflation, but in the long term it should reset itself."

Shawn gave the Professor a quizzical look.

"But you know that there is absolutely no backing. All the Fed is doing is dumping trillions of dollars into the economy simply by printing dollars."

"Yes. This is where things get a little tricky. People

will be more than happy to receive a check in the mail and you know as well as I do that the first several thousand or million people who use that money will not be paying inflationary prices. It will take a few months before the process begins to kick in and we see hyper-inflation."

"But by that time, it will be far too late to stop it. Once those checks are mailed and cashed it will be impossible to stop it."

"Well Shawn, have you considered this: if the government sends out the first few rounds of checks and what we say will happen actually does, then somewhere along the line the government will most likely stop sending out the checks."

"True. And then..." Shawn stopped in mid-sentence.

Suddenly he realized that the Professor had actually thought through the process much further than he had.

"When that happens millions of Americans will protest against the government stopping the payments."

"Exactly. You see, the real problem isn't the fact that all that money is being sent out, the real problem is that it will never *all* be sent out. Look at it his way. You send millions of dollars to middle-class America, let's say those who have a household income of over two-hundred fifty-thousand dollars, and then suddenly stop. Keep in mind that the majority of Americans actually have a household income of less than one-hundred fifty-thousand dollars. Can you see what the end result would be?"

Shawn sat silently for a couple of minutes as his mind worked through to the only possible conclusion. The old man saw the light of recognition in his eyes right before he said:

"Oh my God. When everyone else realizes that they won't be getting any money they will go to the streets against those who did."

"Correct. And you know that, especially in the cities, this will most likely result in violence. Well, you would need to call in the National Guard, the Army, who knows? I highly doubt that the public police force could handle it. Nor do I think that they would want to. In many of these cities the people who would take to the streets are armed with much more powerful weapons than the police are."

"So, what you are saying is that the government *knows* what will happen and is doing it anyways?"

"No, not necessarily. I am saying that if – and it is a big if – the government wants to cause mass riots and violence in the cities then this is one way to accomplish that goal."

"I see. There has to be a way to stop this. Maybe some kind of federal injunction?"

"I doubt that. No judge in his right mind would want to be the one person who denies millions of Americans federal money. Would you want to be the one person who tells everyone 'sorry folks, but the government can't send you any money'? I don't think so."

"So basically, we just wait."

"Yes. We just wait and pray to God that things turn out better than we think."

21

S hawn stayed with the old professor for two days touring the nation's capital and trying to ease his mind. This proved to be a somewhat difficult task as his mind kept returning to the effects of the Stimulus Bill. He felt like a man standing at the edge of disaster wanting to scream at the top of his lungs to warn those around him. Yet every time he looked all he saw were mindless men and women running back and forth searching for the next opportunity to make a dollar. He believed that one person could make a difference, but he also knew that no matter how hard you tried, no matter strong you may be, you could never stop the rising tide.

When Shawn said goodbye to his old friend he did so with a feeling of melancholy. His entire world was turning in directions which, only a few days ago, he would never have thought possible. He wondered if there was anyone else out there who knew what the nation was running towards or who really understood the end results of the new bill. By the time his plane had reached cruising altitude Shawn Reynolds had fallen into a restless sleep.

22

When the Old Professor arrived home, he sat quietly in his study sipping a glass of wine and debating whether to take the next step. It had been years since he was given the gold-plated card with two words stamped in the top. But the words were not what caused him concern, it was the number beneath them. The professor had hoped the day would never come when he might need to make the call, but then his old student and friend had shown up and began to piece together the secret which had been so carefully hidden. No, he did not want to make the call, but the tired old professor knew that they had waited too long and worked too hard to let sentimentality get in the way.

Professor Jonathan Baker lifted his phone and entered the ten-digit number. As the line rang, he quietly said a prayer for his old friend asking Allah to be merciful.

"Greetings Professor."

"Good Evening Rafael. The man knows."

"We will take care of it, old friend."

As the professor ended the call, he felt a sense

of guilt and anguish. John Baker, who was born Joachim Abu' Bakr – had just given his old student and friend a death sentence.

23

Ron dialed the phone and waited for his brother to pick up. After several rings he heard his elder brother's voice.

"This is Phillip Stone. Please leave a message."

"Hey Phillip, this is Ron. I need to ask you a few questions. Could you give me a call when you have a few minutes? Thanks."

Ron hit the end button and tossed the phone on his desk. He let his thoughts wander to when he and Phillip were younger. He remembered how much his older brother seemed so stoic as a child – always lost in thought, never seemingly influenced by emotion. He often thought his brother was strange, but eventually realized that Phillip was just a very thoughtful man who never acted without thinking. That was probably why he excelled in being a mechanic. He loved fixing things that most people couldn't even figure out.

Some things never change, he thought.

24

When Rosa finally awoke from the medicated slumber, she had been in for nearly three weeks, she was met by a young nurse who spoke fluent Spanish.

"Hello there. How do you feel?"

Rosa immediately tensed, wondering if somehow, she had been found and captured.

"It is ok. You are safe. You are at the Phoenix Baptist Hospital. You are in the United States. What is your name?"

"Rosa...Rosa Hernandez."

"Well Rosa, you took a pretty bad fall. Fortunately, a Park Ranger found you and brought you her. You had a pretty bad gash in your head and your left leg was severely broken – the doctors had to put six pins in it to help it heal."

"Thank you," Rosa said in a scratchy voice.

"Here, has some water. It will help your throat. You have been in and out of it for some time because you were given pain killers to help you rest so that your body could begin to heal."

"Yes, thank you."

"Rosa, I will be nearby all day. If you need anything, press this red button and I will come help you, ok?"

"Yes, the red button. Thank you."

As the nurse smiled and walked out the door, Rosa felt a wave of relief pass over her. America? She had always wanted to come to America but could never afford the prices the drug lords charged those who could not come legally. That was when she had met Saul and believed he could rescue her from a life of poverty. Now, it was all too clear what had taken place. Saul was, in fact, not the charming businessman she had thought, but instead was working with the local cartel finding young women and children to turn into mules – people forced in to slavery in order to carry illegal drugs into the United States. These mules were nothing more than tools used by the cartels and, as such, would be discarded and left for dead with no concern by the drivers.

Rosa, by fighting back against her own assailant, had miraculously saved her own life. And now she was safe in America.

Or so she thought she was.

25

With the implementation of the Economic Stimulus Package of 2010, the American economy stalled. After three months the numbers started coming back. Unemployment was creeping up and jobs were being lost by the thousands. Manufacturing in the "Rust Belt" – so-called because it was here that America mined iron ore, made steel, cars, and just about every other manufactured item which required steel -was hit the hardest. Oddly enough most pundits pointed out that Silicon Valley seemed relatively untouched by the slowdown. The talking heads on the three main news networks refused to us the term "recession" as that would cast a dark pall on the current administration.

Every four years there is a Presidential election in the United States. 2012 was no different, with the exception that this time the Republicans chose a moderate candidate who had no chance of winning. The governor from Massachusetts, while seemingly physically fit and good-looking, had simply been too conciliatory. He had presided over the implementation of a single-payer health care plan in his state which, oddly enough, was so similar to the Affordable care Act that many in the nation actually believed it was based upon the Massachusetts law. And while the Governor was intelligent and well-spoken, he was too moderate to energize the conservative base and could not stand up to direct attacks by his opponent. It certainly did not help that his choice for Vice President had betrayed his own party by refusing to implement any fiscally conservative plans he had been elected to pursue.

The election of 2012 was, in the eyes of many, the last-ditch effort by a fading man to reclaim a bit of glory. He simply could not compete with the youth, vitality, and especially the smooth-talking rhetoric of a man who had mastered – better than any President since Ronald Regan – the art of public speaking.

In the end the President won with an electoral victory of 332 -206. What most pundits failed to realize was how close the popular vote was. Here the President won by only five million votes out of nearly 127 million cast. In 2012 the election for the President of the United States was won by less than four percent of the votes cast. Three states helped to determine the outcome, and all three were decided by one or two counties in each. In Ohio – a state no Republican President had ever been elected to office without winning – there are 88 counties. The Democrats won only 17of these, while the Republicans won 71. The difference was that the counties the Democrat candidate won consisted of 56% of the states' population. Similar results were found to be the reason the President won the states of Florida and Pennsylvania.

What most election pundits failed to realize was that in states like Pennsylvania – considered a Democrat stronghold – the Democrat candidate won by only 300,000 votes. All of these votes could be attributed to one county: Philadelphia, which also contains the city by the same name. In this county the Democrats won the popular vote by a count of 588,806 to 96,467, or a margin of 492,339.

The next Republican candidate could easily turn these three states red by simply winning only one county in each. The problem facing the conservative party was how to choose a candidate who could appeal to the so-called "blue color" workers. They would need someone with working experience who could speak the language of the middle class, while having the physical strength to compete during a harsh and often taxing election campaign. Unfortunately for the Republicans, there was really no available nominee who could actually do any of those things.

After the 2012 election the American economy started to slowly improve. As the numbers came in it was obvious to everyone that the rate of growth was the lowest in the nation's history since the Great Depression. While the President could tout that the "economy was growing" he often reminded Americans that the manufacturing jobs lost over the previous years would not be coming back. Americans, he warned, had to adjust to a new type of economy and a new role for the nation on the world stage.

America had entered a malaise similar to that faced during the Carter years. While inflation had not increased as it did during the late 1970's there were indications that prices were increasing, wages were stagnant, and jobs were continuing to leave the nation. The confidence of American in their government was declining to even lower rates than anyone had thought possible.

After nearly eight years of "Hope and Change," America was losing hope and the only changes taking place seemed to benefit the wealthy elites and foreign governments.

26

April 30, 2011 The White House Correspondent's Dinner

On April 30, 2011, the White House Correspondent's Dinner was held in Washington, D.C. On this night it is usual for speakers to hurl comedic insults and jokes at those in attendance. However, on this night two individuals – the President of the United States and a host from a national comedy television program – took great pains to ridicule and insult a powerful and wealthy New York businessman.

During the night the businessman appeared to grow more agitated as the verbal assault continued. While this man had flirted for decades with running for the office of the President of the United States, he had never really taken the idea seriously. However, the uber-competitive nature which had driven this man to amass a fortune of nearly ten billion dollars kicked in. He had conquered nearly everything he had attempted to take on over his sixty-plus years of life. Content with his empire in the more than capable hands of his children, he wanted to take on a more monumental task...and destroying his enemies had always brought a spring in his step and smile to his face.

Slowly he devised his plane for revenge. Slowly he

began to test the waters, to find out what it would take to win. And he began to realize that, in order for people like him to continue to be successful and for the people of this nation to have the opportunity to move forward, someone had to challenge these elites who had nearly driven the US economy into a never-ending hole.

On this night, the wealthy billionaire, who owned dozens of properties around the world, hosted the most popular show on television, and who had tirelessly worked his entire life to build an empire he could leave to his children and the thousands of people who lives he had enriched through employment opportunities which would not even exist without him, made what to him was an easy decision.

He would run for President of the United States. No holds barred. Hands free. Total commitment.

For most Americans, the most important issue when it comes to Presidential elections is economic growth. Americans want to know that the opportunities they have are getting better – not worse. From 2012 – 2105 the average GPD rate of growth was 2.35%. While this may seem good, it was – in fact – less than the average rate the United States experienced since the Great Depression. From 1939 – 2016 there were several years which saw over 7% GDP growth. To be fair, there were years where the GPD rate was negative. The worst year of negative GPD growth since the Great Depression took place in 2009 – the first year of President Barak Obama's first term in office. The rate of growth was an astonishing -2.54%. From that year the rate grew – but at a slower rate than any year since the Great Depression. In his last year in office, President Obama oversaw a rate of economic growth of negative 1.31%.

27

June 16, 2015 – New York City

As the businessman came down the escalator he waved to a large crowd of supporters. His wife – herself a legal immigrant who spoke several languages and had amassed her own fortune – was beside him. His children were also present. He stepped off the last moving stair and confidently strode to the podium set up for this occasion.

He spoke with a strength and honesty which had been missing in Washington, DC for decades:

"So, I've watched the politicians. I've dealt with them all my life, if you can't make a good deal with a politician then there is something wrong with you, you certainly aren't very good, and that's what we have representing us. They will never make America great again. They don't even have a chance. They're controlled fully by the lobbyists, by the donors, and by the special interests fully – that's who controls them. Hey, I have lobbyists, I have lobbyists who can produce anything for me, but you know what? It won't happen, because we have to stop doing things for some people, but for this country – it's destroying this

country - we have to stop, and we have to stop now.

Our country needs a truly great leader and we need that now. We need a leader that can bring back our jobs, can bring back our manufacturing, can bring back our military, can bring back our vets – our vets have been abandoned. We need somebody who can take the brand of the United States and make it great again – it's not great again.

We need somebody that literally will take this country and make it great again, we can do that. I can tell you I love my life. I have a wonderful family. You know, all of my life I have heard that a truly successful person cannot run for public office; and yet that is the kind of mind-set you need to make this country great again.

So, ladies and gentlemen, I am officially running for President of the United States and we are going to make our country great again."

Within five minutes every major television network was reporting the story in a negative light. A man who was once lauded by the NAACP as a hero to Black America, was now called racist. A man who took pictures with the likes of Civil Rights icons Rosa Parks, Al Sharpton, and Jesse Jackson was now – according to the MSM – a white supremacist who was fighting to subjugate and destroy blacks in America.

On day one the attacks against the businessman's character went viral – along with numerous claims by pundits and comedians alike that there was absolutely no chance for this man, one of the hardest working men in America, to win the Presidency – let alone the nomination from his party.

America, it seemed, had much different plans.

28

November 7ᵗʰ, 2016

T he Democrat nominee squealed in excitement as the early returns seemed to be in her favor. So certain of victory had she and her party been that in the last three weeks leading up to the election she failed to make any campaign stops in Pennsylvania or even Michigan – both historically parts of the so-called "rust-belt" which Democrats had dominated for over sixty years.

As the evening continued the vote tally seemed to be shifting slightly in favor of the opposition candidate. No worries, she told herself, we have planned for this.

At nearly midnight of November 7ᵗʰ, 2016, it became apparent that the Democrat nominee for President of the United States was going to lose. She had no idea how this could happen. As she stepped into the back-stage room her anger came out in a sudden burst of vulgarity and violence.

She slammed the door, slapped her husband – a former President himself – and screamed at the top of her lungs.

"We had this! How could this, this THING beat us? We paid good money for that dossier – it should have ruined him. And what about all of the false sexual allegations? Hell, he didn't wet his whistle one hundredth of the times YOU did! How in the world did all of our disinformation fail?"

What she failed to understand – what they all failed to understand – was that working-class America had reached its full of Washington politics. For nearly eighty years the American people had been voting for politicians who promised them that things would get better; that a brighter day was just around the corner. It had almost worked twice – once, in 1960 with the election of John Kennedy. Unfortunately for him, and America, his desire to expose both the Federal Reserve system as the corrupt institution it was, and the CIA for the many illegal actions it had been behind for decades, had cost him his life – when he was assassinated in Dallas on November 22, 1963.

The second time the American people came close to "draining the swamp" came in 1980, when Ronald Reagan was elected. This man also planned to expose the Federal Reserve and to severely limit or even stop the illegal assassinations by the CIA. He too, however, was nearly killed when an assassination attempt occurred on March 30th, 1981. This time the so-called Deep State did not wait three years to send their message.

In 2016 – in spite of numerous disinformation campaigns and false allegations – America chose a man to be President who was the one thing they had been looking for: he was not a politician.

This victory for the American people rocked the Deep State and the Globalists who controlled Washington, D.C., the banking industry, and the Main Stream Media. However, it was not these groups that truly pulled the strings. No, there was a deeper, darker group who truly controlled the powers of America...and they were as stunned as any that the New York Businessman had won.

29

Roger Caldwell walked out of the Javits Center in New York City shaking his head.

"How did this happen, Stephen? I thought you were going to make certain the Russian thing was our ace-in-the-hole?"

"I am sorry, sir. All of our analysts assured me that connecting the President-elect with Russia would guarantee us victory. We even paid that porn star to make those false claims. I really do not understand what happened."

"Enough. It is apparent that these, while decent attempts, were not the problem. I believe the candidate herself was the problem. I was not convinced that the wife of a former President – especially one so mired in sexual deviance as he is – was the best choice, Stephen."

"Yes, sir, but it was her time. She had been a faithful servant to us."

"Ha! Servant? She has been more of a thorn in my side for decades. Her entire life she has been looking out for nothing more than what can be done for her. Hell, she even married a man who can't keep his pants on just to gain political power and money. No, Stephen, she has never been for us. She is nothing more than a broken tool to be discarded."

"Yes, sir. Shall I call Rafael?"

"No. We have waited a long time, Stephen. Four more years is but a drop of water in the ocean. No, we will simply change our focus. I want a meeting, Stephen. A meeting with everyone."

"Yes, sir."

30

Four days later.

T he men seated around the table came from all over the world. They included members of royal families, the heads of the largest corporations of the world, as well as the leaders of some of the most influential social media platforms. They had gathered at the request of the man who controlled them all: Roger Caldwell.

As Roger Caldwell looked around the table, he saw the twelve men – "heads" he thought of them - heads of the twelve different "zones" he had created in his mind to help him achieve his goals. Each one represented one area of expertise he needed in order to usher in the "Grand Vision" as they called it. Most people knew it under a different name: The New World Order.

An order, unbeknownst to most, that originated on a small island off the coast of Georgia, in 1910.

31

Jekyll Island, Georgia, November, 1910

A light mist covered the grounds of the train station like a gray blanket. The man standing alone at the central doors smiled and spoke quietly to himself.

"All the better. It actually looks and feels like hunting weather."

Nelson W. Aldrich was born in Foster, Rhode Island, to fairly average middle-class parents. Aldrich's life was one of boredom and regularity until he joined the Union Army in May, 1862. He saw no combat, as his regiment was part of the larger force designated to defend the nation's capital, Washington, D.C. He was mustered out in September of the same year and returned, once again, to a rather mundane existence. Aldrich's life took a turn when he married Abigail Truman.

Aldrich became involved in politics after a brief tour of Europe in 1872, where he spent time figuring out his purpose in life after the death of a child. Upon his return, he was elected to several local and states offices, catching the eyes of the Rhode Island Republican Party political bosses. It was customary in the late 1800's for politicians seeking national office to be "selected" by the state political machines as this would ensure their willingness to promote the party business.

Aldrich won election to the United States House of Representatives in 1878. He would serve only one term. In 1881 he was chosen by the Rhode Island state legislature to represent the state in the US Senate – where he would serve for the next thirty years.

Aldrich had eleven children – most notable was his daughter, Abigail Greene Aldrich, who would marry John D. Rockefeller, Jr., and give birth to Nelson Aldrich Rockefeller – a four-term governor of New York who would famously – and unsuccessfully - run for President four times. Nelson would, however, be appointed Vice-President of the United States by President Gerald Ford in 1974. Aldrich's first daughter – Lucy – would go on to a fairly forgotten life. She would have four children – three daughters and a son, whose name was Roger Aldrich Caldwell.

As Aldrich scanned the coast line of south-east Georgia, he saw a man step out of a railway car and stride over to where he stood.

"Good morning, Piatt. How are you?"

"Quite well Nelson. Good day for hunting, isn't it?" the man said with a wicked grin.

"Why, yes. Yes, it is. If you could hop aboard my private line it will take you to the island."

"Are we all together then?"

"No. You will each travel separately in order to prevent any of the locals from seeing us as a group. I need this to be as secretive as possible for now. I thought you were informed of this?"

"Ah, yes, well...I was just making sure Nelson. One can never be too careful about these things."

"Good day then, sir. The others should be arriving soon."

"Good day."

As Piatt – whose name was Abram Piatt Andrew, Jr. – stepped aboard the short but elegant private train, he did not notice the man in a dark suit watching him from the second story window of the train station. Standing just inside the window was the man whose idea had started the motions for this highly secretive meeting: John Pierpont Morgan. Morgan controlled the nation's banks, as well as being heavily involved in some of the world's first multinational corporations.

Morgan was here to make sure that Aldrich did exactly as he was told – and he was told to create a banking system that could be controlled by a private corporation which was not accountable to either the people of the United States or their representatives.

Aldrich would succeed.

32

As Roger Caldwell looked around the table, he saw the twelve men – "heads" he thought of them - heads of the twelve different "zones" he had created in his mind to help him achieve his goals. Each one represented one area of expertise he needed in order to usher in the "Grand Vision" as they called it. Most people knew it under a different name: The New World Order.

"Gentlemen, I have called this meeting in order to discuss a rather unexpected event. As most of you know our chosen candidate, for whatever reason, was unable to achieve the task we selected her for. That being the case, we must work to be certain our ultimate goals can still be achieved."

A young man – young by Caldwell's standards – spoke with a slight British accent:

"Can't we simply arrange for Rafael to have a meeting with the new President?"

"No, your highness, I think three times in sixty years would be a bit much for even the American people to take. They may be as sheep led to the slaughter, but there are still enough bulls among them to cause problems."

This time it was the Middle-Easterner who spoke:

"Mr. Caldwell, surely you can find something to use against this man? After all, he is just a man."

"No, your eminence, we have already tried that. As you know, we released several false stories about extramarital affairs – all which led nowhere. We are, however, looking at moving in a different direction. I believe Stephen can explain."

Stephen Hammonds stood up. He was always nervous when addressing this group. He could stand in front of ten thousand shareholders and not break a sweat...but, for some reason, standing in front of these thirteen men made feel as if the weight of the world was bearing down upon his soul, not that he believed he had a soul.

"Gentlemen, there are two major concerns we are faced with. First, since our candidate did not win, we are unable to move forward at this time with our vision. I am confident, however, in the plan we have to ensure victory in the next election. Second, in order to ensure the plan can move forward we need to have the right person in office. This person must be willing to enact every policy we need in order to achieve success."

"Great. But how do you propose we ensure our man gets selected next time? The previous choice should have utterly destroyed her competition," asked the man with the British accent.

"Yes, well, there is a three-phase plan I have created that will, in my opinion, give us as sure an outcome as possible. I do not see it failing."

"I think you Americans are too soft. In my empire we simply execute those who oppose true leadership," added the Middle-Eastern leader.

Roger Caldwell spoke up:

"Please, gentlemen, let's not forget. We have tried in the past to use violence to destroy the world's economy. My father thought the Great War would work. That failed. Then, we thought the depravity of the Great Depression would work. Well, as we all know, things became too bad for any economy to be successful. Why do you think we put Hitler in power? And he nearly succeeded! I told you – nothing can be achieved through violence. When the American people are pushed too far, they will ultimately fight back. And they have been able to stop us every time. No, we must find a way to make the people themselves believe they are choosing to go in this direction. Granted, even I thought the Cloward-Piven strategy would work, but that was too controversial. The American people love their freedom. Hence, we must make them believe that they are choosing to accept our vision. It cannot be forced upon them."

Stephen continued:

"I have developed this three-phase plan to be implemented over the course of the next four years. Assuming it is executed properly, I cannot see how it will fail."

"And what are those three steps?"

"We have plans in place to direct the opposition party to begin impeachment proceedings against the

President. This will cast even more doubt upon his ability to lead. This will keep the President on the defensive until we can begin the second phase."

"And what is that?" asked the representative from the Far East.

"There are two parts that will work in conjunction with each other. The first is the release of a bioweapon we have been working on with both the head of the American National Institute of Health and the Wuhan Institute of Virology. We believe that, in conjunction with a mass media declaration that this as a worldwide pandemic, and the ability of our media friends to silence dissent, we can create a situation where fear of the virus will become more important to the American people than any other issue."

At this point Stephen looked at the young, readheaded man and asked: "Are you ready to engage?"

"Yes. I can easily ban or, at the minimum, call into question any post or article that does not support our narrative."

"Good. Now, the last part will involve the election itself. We have recently come into controlling interest in a company that makes the voting machines which will be used in several states. We are assured that the results can easily be influenced in the direction of our desired choice. Also, we are hoping to use the pandemic scare as a way to influence the outcome also."

"This seems all fine and dandy," said the Brit, "but I still don't see how you can convince the American people that their election isn't rigged."

At this point Roger Caldwell spoke up.

"The American Presidential election has been rigged for well over a hundred years. The only time it was ever really close was in 1960 when Kennedy defeated Nixon. While Nixon was our choice, it was made very clear to him not to contest the election. We had more than enough on the Kennedy family to control them."

"And how did that work out?" retorted a man dressed in traditional African garb.

"I think we all know what happened. It is no secret to the men gathered here that Oswald was, in fact, a patsy. That did actually turn out for the best. This is when we realized how simple it was to control the narrative by using the American mass media."

Caldwell rubbed the sides if his head. It was becoming difficult to teach these men and make them understand the importance of patience. Ah, patience, something his father has often told him was the most important part of a man's character. He often remembered the lesson.

"It may take years, or it may take decades, Roger. However, with patience it will happen. Remember, we serve a power that knows no bounds of time. Be patient, son, and perhaps you will see the fulfillment of his vision."

Time and time again, Roger had to remind himself that this had been planned for over a hundred years, what was another four years? But, to be so close. To actually be able to see the finish line. Roger wanted so much to be the one who would see the fulfillment of the vision. Yet, here he was, having to look after this rabble like a school teacher in a class of ungrateful children.

"You have all agreed to partake in the vision. Need I remind you that it takes time. Every set-back is nothing more than another lesson to learn; another pathway to take. We cannot become rash when we are this close. What is four years to a thousand?"

The men all shook their heads in agreement.

As the last man left the room, Roger Caldwell beckoned to Stephen.

"Stephen, please make the calls. Also, I want you to be certain that Western Europe and the United States are affected by the virus to the maximum degree possible. Make sure the media plays this up as the worst pandemic in human history."

"Yes, sir."

With that, Roger Caldwell stepped to the elevator and looked around. So close. So very, very close. Now, all that was needed was to find a man who could be both easily controlled and, if needed, be easily removed. He had someone in mind. An old college friend who had become wealthy as both an American Senator and then Vice-President. Yes, Roger thought to himself, he will do just fine. He had heard that the man was showing the early signs of dementia. This would be perfect. Easily controlled yet able to be dispatched quickly if the need arose.

Roger Caldwell pressed the S5 button on the elevator and, as the doors silently closed, he let out a deep sigh.

"Perfect."

33

Selma Hernandez smiled. After a long recovery from her ordeal, and with the help of the local Catholic Charities, she had found a new home in a small Colorado town. The local church helped her find a job as a waitress at a local truck stop. The people in the small town had openly accepted her and she quickly made several friends, mostly other waitresses and truckers who passed through. She had just begun her eight-hour shift when she noticed two men walk in and sit down near the back.

"So, Phillip, what do you think?" asked Tom.

"Well, I like the guy. He's not a politician, so that's good. I mean, those guys have run our country into the ground."

"Yeah, but do you think any of those things they say are true?"

"Nah man. This guy has been on the front page of every newspaper in the country, on every magazine, AND he had a number one television show. Don't you think that if any of this is true it would have come out before now? No, I'm telling you, it's politicians. They are worried about him. He will expose all of them for the fraud they are."

"Yeah, I guess so."

"Listen, you can't trust the media anyway. Remember, they were the ones that told us we could keep our insurance and our doctors too. Well, all I can say is I lost my doctor because the company couldn't afford the increase in premiums. Hell, we had to pay a fine that was more than we were paying in insurance!"

Phillip thought back over the past several years. His had lost his job – as had every worker in the plant – when the company he worked for decided to move to Mexico in order to save on labor costs and taxes. He hoped this new guy could help out. After all, he had campaigned on bringing manufacturing jobs back, and his brother, who worked in Detroit at the Ford factory, had already been re-hired when Ford decided to not move a truck factory. That had been done at the request of the President.

"So, you hear old man Sheppard passed? Couple months ago, I guess."

Phillip knew. He remembered the meeting the old man had led. Such excitement it seemed was running through the community back then. But life catches up to everyone and things seemed to settle down after the initial fervor. Seems like that was always the case. Something happened, everyone got in a tussle, and then it just faded away and life went on. Eight long years of not knowing if things would ever get better. Would he be able to leave a better country for his kids just like his father had done for him? He often wondered, but with the election of the new President – a man who loved America and fought for her every day – he saw a glimmer of hope. Maybe, just maybe, this man could bring back American greatness and reinvigorate those who believed in the exceptionalism of this land.

"Well," Phillip said, "it kind of sucks. I liked that guy – he had some big ones. Never afraid to speak his mind, was he?"

"Nah, but he was a little crazy, ya know? I mean, did he really think he could lead some kind of revolution? That was just nuts man. Nobody can stand up against the government."

"Well, maybe we won't have to. This new guy, I like him. He is already fighting for us. I don't remember anyone in Washington ever looking out for the small guy."

Selma returned and filled up both men's coffee.

"Hey Selma, how's it going?"

"Good. How are you?"

"I can't complain. You think this new guy is going to help us out? Would be nice if the factory could open back up."

"Can't say. I think he means well, but I learned a long time ago to wait for results. I hope he does make things better. If America does not survive, there will be no place on earth for people to escape to. I know I would probably be dead if I didn't have America."

"Yeah, well, that's what is so great about her. People can come her and start over. Begin a new life, and if you work hard and stay out of trouble, you can maybe make it big! I mean, look at us – who could have imagined that two knuckleheads would be so wealthy and happy! Heck, I might just spring for another cup!"

All three laughed as Selma topped off the cups and walked back to the counter. She understood better than most how important it was for the United States to remain the beacon of freedom she had been for so long, to so many. She knew her words rang truer than people realized. If America descended into Socialism and chaos, there would be no place on earth for the oppressed to seek true refuge.

34

T he President hung up the phone. He had just spent about fifteen minutes speaking with the newly elected Ukrainian President.

"I hope he is successful. That place had been run by some really bad people, I mean, really bad. I think he wants what's best for his people, at least to follow thew law and let the people live free. That's great."

The National Security Advisor agreed.

"Yes, sir. Mr. Chelensky is a law-and-order guy. I am pretty sure he will work on rooting out the corruption. At least, that is what our assets tell us."

"Good, good. Listen, we need to be sure that his administration is on the up and up before we release those funds. We will no longer give aid to corrupt politicians. As soon as we have confirmation that he is legit, let's make sure he gets his money."

"And what about Cloudstrike? What do you want to do there?"

"Nothing. It is his country. I just want to make

sure that the corruption of the previous administration hasn't continued over to the new one. Listen, we can't have American politicians making money off of their corrupt contacts overseas. That stops now. If he finds that it was all good, then fine, we move on. If, however, we find that there was a misuse of an American politician – or his family – specifically for the purpose of making personal financial gain at the cost of the tax payers...well, we need to know these things."

"Alright. I will keep up with it."

"Good. Now, what's next on the schedule?"

35

Two days later the tall man walked into the office of the Speaker of the House of Representatives and placed a manilla envelope on the secretary's desk.

"Please be sure that the Speaker is able to look at this today."

"Yes sir. May I ask who is leaving it?"

"Just tell the speaker that a friend of the American people has some interesting information for her."

Later that day the Speaker was going through her mail when she noticed the thin manilla envelope. There were no marks in it so she was not aware of where it had come from.

She pressed the button on her phone and waited a moment for the connection to be made.

"Yes, ma'am?" came the reply from her secretary.

"Do you know what this manilla envelope is doing on my desk? I don't recall requesting anything."

"Yes, ma'am. It was brought in earlier today by a man who simply said he was a friend of the American people. I had security check it out. There are no chemicals or powders present and it passed the x-ray test."

"I see. A friend of the American people, you said?"

"Yes ma'am. That is what he called himself."

"Thank you."

With that the Speaker ended the call and sank down into her four-thousand-dollar chair. She had forgotten about the man who had shown up in her office unbidden several years ago. Now she wondered what he wanted. A cold chill ran through her as she opened up the envelope and pulled out the single sheet of paper. After quickly reading through it, she again pressed the button summoning her secretary into her office.

"Get me the Senate Minority leader on the phone right now."

"Yes, ma'am."

About ten minutes went by before she heard the phone ring. Took her long enough, she thought to herself.

"Hello, Chuck?"

"Yes. What do you need?"

"I need a face-to-face with you as soon as possible. I think we have something and I want to run it by you."

"What is it?"

"Well, if I wanted to tell you on the phone, I wouldn't have asked to see you in person, would I? Just get over here!"

She slammed the phone down and cussed out loud. That idiot from New York just didn't get it. He was the minority leader in the Senate. A pretty worthless job and one he seemed suited for. She, on the other hand, was the Speaker of the House. Third in line for the Presidency. That idiot in the other chamber needed to learn his place – again. And she would be certain that this time he would understand who really held the power.

As the Senator from New York closed the door to the Speaker's inner office, he was handed the single sheet of paper the Speaker had been given.

"What is this?"

"This, you idiot, is the key to destroying that moron in the White House."

"Oh. I see. A phone call. You want to ruin him over a call congratulating the President-elect of the Ukraine? Seriously?"

"Just shut up and sit down. Listen, there is going to be a whistle-blower report filed in three days – I have made sure of that. In this report it will be alleged that the President used his power to threaten the new Ukrainian President."

"Really? Was this whistle-blower present when the call was made?"

"It doesn't matter. Hell, it doesn't even matter if it is true. All that matters is that there is a whistle-blower who claims the President made a *quid pro quo* with the leader of another nation. We can spin this like an Oklahoma tornado. The media will eat this up. Then it won't matter what the truth is."

"So, you want to go after the President over a call that was totally legitimate because some staffer who wasn't even present thinks he might have overheard someone else say something he didn't like?"

"No. We are going after the President because he is an idiot who refuses to work with us. This man needs to be ruined and we need to make sure that in 2020 we can win. Look, the truth doesn't matter. Just get it out in the media and they will repeat it often enough that it will become the truth."

"A *quid pro quo*? You really think that will work? If I remember correctly, didn't the former Vice President admit to threatening the previous Ukrainian President with a *quid pro quo*? Nothing happened with that. What makes you think this will be any different?"

"This will be different because the current President is not one of us. The last guy, regardless of how idiotic he is, was one of us. The media doesn't care what we do, as long as they get their quotes and sound bites. They hate this new guy as much as we do."

"I see. Well, whatever you want, I can see what I can do on my end."

Probably nothing, the Speaker thought. This man had lost the Senate and was too stupid to figure out how to use the media to get it back. She, on the other hand, knew how to manipulate the media to do her bidding. Not that it was really so hard. The American media had long been in the pocket of the Liberal establishment.

"Listen, you just make sure that when it gets over to you, you have all your people ready to eviscerate this man. I don't care if there is evidence or not. The news will line up with us like they always do."

With that she dismissed the Minority Leader. And gladly. She hated the she had to work with a person who was less of a man than she was. Some day she had to look into getting him replaced. Soon, maybe, but until then she would have to keep him in line.

36

Wuhan Institute of Virology, Wuhan,
China, November 3rd, 2019

T he call came in early in the morning. Deputy Director Glunge thought it was odd that a call would be so early. Generally, the Party Committee Secretary did not arrive until after eight.

"Hello?"

"Director Glunge?"

"Yes. This is he."

"Director, please stay on the line for a call from the Chairman."

The Chairman? Why was the Chairman of the Communist Party calling? And what did he want with him? Director Glunge nervously waited the two minutes it took for the call to connect.

"Hello. Is this Director Glunge?"

"Yes sir. Well, I am the Deputy Director. How may I help you?"

"Deputy Director? Well, after today you will be

the person who will be running the lab. You will be receiving instructions from the local Deputy of the Party Committee. It is imperative that you follow them exactly. Do you understand?"

"Yes sir. May I ask what this involves?"

"Do not concern yourself. It is the will of the Party and you will either follow your directive or you will be replaced. Do you understand?"

"Yes. Yes, I understand."

"Good. Remember, you must do exactly as you are told. No deviations will be tolerated. Need I remind you that failure to follow Party directives will not look good for you or your family."

"Yes, sir. I understand."

With that the line went dead and the Deputy Director of the Wuhan Institute of Virology sat down and waited for the man who could help him become the true director of the lab he had prepared his entire professional life for. But why would the Chairman of the Party take such a personal interest? No matter, he thought. If it helped him advance, he didn't care what was required. And this might even get him noticed by the people in Beijing.

37

As the Chairman hung up the phone, he pulled out a small card that was faded and worn. There was nothing on the card except a phone number. A number he though we would never use. The time had come, evidently, for him to make the one call he had been wanting to make for decades.

Roger Caldwell picked up the forest green headset – he really loved that color – and listened to the Chinese Communist Party Chairman.

"I have begun the process. The virus will be released into a local fish market as well as to twenty-five businessmen who will be travelling to Europe and the United States over the next two weeks."

"Good." Roger said. "Are you sure this cannot be traced back to either the Party or the Lab?"

"Will all due respect, Mr. Caldwell, I control the state media. They will report what I tell them to."

"And what of the World Health Organization?"

"I am not worried about those fools. China will claim that the virus is a natural occurrence and that we have it under control. The World Health Organization will do what we tell them. That organization has no courage and will bend like a reed in the wind."

"Good. How long before this will reach America?"

"I would give it a month. It will take a few days to spread in the market and at least a week before it can reach Europe and America. After that we simply let it take its natural course."

"I see. And how deadly is this virus, Chairman?"

"According to my scientists it is no deadlier that the normal flu. I may be slightly more dangerous to the elderly and weak, but there is nothing for us to concern ourselves with. With proper nutrition and health, the chances of a person dying form this is nearly zero."

"Well, thank you. Remember, however, that this must be seen as a deadly disease."

"Yes, I will have our media report that from day one."

"Good. Thank you."

As Roger Caldwell hung up the phone he smiled. So, it is beginning. The next step is to make certain that both the media and the politicians in Washington are on board. Of course, that was the easy part. All you had to do was throw money at the politicians and they would fall in line. The Media was even easier. Give them a story and they would run with it as far as they could. Pulitzer had taught him that one.

It seemed that it was all falling in line. It was nearly too easy he thought. But that was when he needed to be at his best. Too many times in the past it had seemed too easy. And just as easily the plans they had put together fell apart because of one man. It was amazing how just one man could literally ruin years of planning and hard work. This time, however, he was sure that the one man who could derail his plans would not. This was why he had spent so much time planning.

38

January 19, 2020 – Snohomish County, Washington

T he man sat in the clinic office wearing a cheap mask. He had been coughing for three days and had developed a fever as well. He had decided to seek medical help because he had heard of a new virus that originated in Wuhan, China. The same place he had just spent two weeks visiting family. He thought back to the trip and could not remember coming into contact with anyone who seemed sick. Perhaps it was the plane trip? He did remember sitting next to a man who claimed he was travelling on business from China to the United States. While there were no red flags that caught his attention, he did remember that the man had spent a good deal of time coughing. He would have to wait for the attendant to give him the test. Hopefully it was just the Flu – but one could never be sure.

As the technician read the results of the test, she was somewhat puzzled. The patient showed all the symptoms of the common flu yet had tested negative for both the A and the B strands. The patient also tested negative for the four most common coronavirus strands which affected humans. She decided to send the specimen to the CDC for further evaluation. She made sure to contact the state department of health as well as the county agency – just in case. Lastly, she noted that the patient had recently been in China, near a city called Wuhan, where he was visiting family members. Wuhan...she thought to herself. She remembered that name from somewhere but could not remember where she had heard it before. It was probably in some report issued. She would get these four or five times a week – each one warning of some new catastrophic disease about to break out. Well, she couldn't really concern herself with that now; there were still eleven other people to see today and she wanted to get home early and spend some time with her three-year-old.

The technician filed the paperwork, sent the patient home with some aspirin and told him to rest. If the symptoms worsened, he should go to the emergency room.

39

Stephen Hammonds picked up the phone and dialed the number again. This time he would have good news for Roger, he hoped.

"Hello Stephen, how are you?"

"Good, sir. You?"

"Ah, well, time will tell. Any news for me?"

"Yes sir. I have just been notified by our man in the CDC that the first case of the Wuhan virus has been identified in the United States. We can estimate that the spread will increase slowly at first and then pick-up pace as we enter the early Spring."

"Good. We need to make sure that no alarms are sounded for at least a month or two. Let's give it time to get out there before we make any announcements."

"Yes sir. I have spoken with Dr. Fredrich and he assures me that he can keep this under wraps for at least a month, maybe longer. It will really depend on the CDC."

"Good. Keep me informed."

With that the connection ended and Stephen felt

relief flow through him. Finally, he could rest a moment knowing that their plan had begun to move ever so closer. Soon it would pick up speed and become unstoppable. Now, if only that fool in the White House didn't mess things up.

40

January 31, 2020. The Oval Office, Washington, D.C.

T he President sat at the Resolute Desk – an old wooden desk made from the salvaged timber of the HMS Resolute – the desk was a gift from Queen Victoria to President Rutherford B. Hayes in 1880 – rubbing his chin. He was deep in thought after hearing from the head of the CDC concerning a new virus that had recently been discovered. The virus was a coronavirus – according to the CDC, non-lethal to most people – yet highly contagious. The President was considering a course of action to take. While his medical advisors assured him that the virus was no more dangerous than the common flu, the President also understood that novelty of the virus and the fact that there was really no data to determine just how deadly or contagious it might be.

"So," the President said, "all we really know is that this is a new type of virus? We don't have any idea how deadly or contagious it might be?"

Dr. Fredrich, the head of the National Institute of Health's Infectious Disease Department, responded.

"Correct, sir. All we really know is that it presents

similar to influenza. It is most likely only dangerous to the elderly and those with underlying conditions which affect the heart and lungs. We don't have any specific data other than that at this time."

"I see. What are the effects this had in China?"

"Well, sir, all we really know is that it was spreading fairly quickly, but the Chinese have been able to contain it."

"And how trustworthy is this information?"

"All I can tell you is that is what the Chinese state media is reporting. We aren't being allowed to get feet on the ground in Wuhan, nor has China allowed either the WHO or the International Red Cross access. I can tell you that it appears to be significantly more contagious than either influenza strain or any of the other coronavirus strains."

"Ok. Well, what is your suggestion?"

"Sir, I think it is best that we just give it time to see how it develops. There have been no serious cases reported, so for now it is really just a kind of super flu."

"Right. A super flu that might be significantly dangerous to our elderly population. And China seems to be hiding any and all information we would need in order to make a better determination as to how to proceed."

"It would seem that way. Let me caution you though. With no data we can't be certain how this virus will act. Certainly, we don't want to cause any wide spread panic."

"Right. So, our choices are to sit and wait while we rely upon what is most likely false information from China, or we can take proactive steps to try and slow the spread."

"That is correct."

"Ok, so again, what is your *professional* opinion?"

"From a purely medical perspective, I suggest we just wait and see how things develop."

"I see. Ok, well, thank you."

The infectious disease expert stood up and was escorted out by one of the President's staffers. When he reached his office across the street, he picked up his phone and dialed the number on the old, worn card.

"Hello. What do you have to report?"

"I believe I convinced him to do nothing for now. We probably have a month or two before he would act on anything."

"Good. Thank you. I will let the council know."

41

The Oval Office

L isten, I don't trust the Chinese," said the President. "If this virus was as weak as they claim then there would be no need to hide it from us."

The President's Chief of staff chimed in, "Sir, I think Dr. Fredrich is right on this. There just isn't enough data to justify any response at this time. We would get hammered by the press and the Democrats if we even looked at this right now."

"Sure, because the media and the Democrats haven't been hammering me over that fake Russia crap for three years? No, my gut tells me there is more to this virus than we are being told."

The President leaned back in his chair and thought to himself for a few minutes. He finally decided what he was going to do, knowing that the media and opposition would probably try to use even this against him.

"Ok, here is what we will do. First, I want a travel ban to and from China for all persons except American citizens. Second, let's hold a press conference informing the people of this new virus and assuring them it is not a serious threat – that we are only taking preliminary precautions to help minimize the spread until we learn mor about it. Third, I want a meeting with the leadership of both houses to discuss where we can go from here. Am I clear?"

"Yes, sir. But, are you sure this is the best course of action?" asked the Chief of Staff.

"Yes. The primary job of every President is to protect the American people from any threat out there. This may prove to be nothing, but I will not take the chance that a so-called super virus is out there and, knowing I had the chance to take action, did nothing because of a politically appointed hack."

"Sir, I wouldn't call Dr. Fredrich a political hack."

"I would. He was appointed to his job by the swamp and has been there for over twenty years. His advice is designed to be the most politically neutral possible. Listen, these swamp creatures care about two things, one: keeping power, and two: making money. And the way they do that is to never commit to anything. I experienced this first-hand when I was doing business in New York. They all wanted donations to their campaigns and would give you the sweet talk, but none of them – not one – would ever make a commitment to you. And I mean it didn't matter who you were or what party they belonged to. No, my job is to protect the people of this nation and if it upsets those talking heads on television, so be it."

"Do I make myself clear?"

"Yes, sir."

The room was completely silent as every person realized that the President was deadly serious. He had already proven that he would fight for the people no matter the personal cost. This is why he donated his entire salary to charity. He had worked his entire life for himself, his family, his business, and his employees. Now he wanted to give back to the nation that had given him so much.

"I want to be absolutely clear on this. No travel to or from China, except for citizens, until we fully understand this virus. I don't care what the media or the opposition party says or does. Hell, I don't care what members of our party say. We don't work for them. We work for the American people. All of the American people. Understood?"

Every person nodded in agreement.

As the Chief of staff left the Oval Office, he shook his head. He hoped the President was making the right decision. He always hoped he was. He had never met a man who loved his country so much. He often wondered if the American people truly understood just how deeply rooted the President's passion for America was? How could he get that message across? With a campaign to run and an election looming, the man had to walk a fine line. He understood that the President would not sacrifice his duty for political gain, yet he also understood that in order to make the changes which were so vitally necessary, they would need those four more years.

42

T he Speaker sat quietly as the man spoke. She could sit for hours without showing any outward emotion. However, today she had a thin smile on her ragged face. She was planning on more than just winning the election – she had dreams of being the President herself. And with the choice her party made for President and Vice President, she was sure that she could manipulate her way to the Oval Office. She just needed a little help. The man speaking might just give her that help.

"So, a pandemic will allow us to send out literally hundreds of millions of votes. The more important part, though, is that we have now convinced nearly the entire population that it is dangerous to vote in person. This will allow us to do three things. First, mail-in ballots. These are easily manipulated. As we receive them, we simply wait until the day after the election to count them."

"Why?" asked the Speaker.

"Well, waiting until after the election does two

things. One, it makes sure than all the people who show up in person are no longer idling around and watching. Two, it makes it much easier for us in major cities to discard ballots cast for our opponent."

"I see. What about the machines?"

"I will get to that. Now, after mail-in ballots we have a secondary plan in place. We can make sure that the voting machines in major cities – at least in all the so-called swing states – have a software update the day before the election. This will put a small program in place to automatically switch about five percent of the votes cast for the President to our guy. This is done at the root level of the software, so there will be very little evidence. All we need to do is make sure that we can shut down the machines for about an hour or two."

"Fine, but how do you prevent anyone from finding out?"

"Well, the data will be sent to a server in Germany where it will be manipulated and then sent back. This is why we need the hour or so. The data has to travel, be received, changed, and then sent back. This will, we estimate, take about ninety minutes."

"I see."

"Also, we can shut down the counting locations. When we shut them down, we are prepared to bring in tens of thousands of ballots for our candidate. Since there will only be our people there it should be fairly quick and easy."

"How will you prevent the opposition from

watching?"

"Don't worry, we have the governors and the courts on our side. Also, the media will report whatever we want them to. We simply report that this is all a conspiracy theory and that there is no evidence of fraud. The media will eat that up."

"No evidence? There will be fraud taking place right in front of the entire world!"

"Madam Speaker, it doesn't matter what people see. All that matters is what the media tells them. Our supporters are fanatical. If we told them the sky was red, they would believe that. Don't worry, the media is our friend."

With that the man left the Speakers' office. The Representative from California sat and thought to herself. "It can't really be that easy, can it?" And yet, it was so easy to convince the media that a fake intelligence report from a has-been English spy was actually written by the Russians and was intended to help the President win in 2016. What fools the American people were. To actually believe a lie when all the evidence pointed to her own party was too simplistic.

"Oh, well," she said out loud, "If the American people will let us impeach a President over a phone call that was totally legitimate, then they deserved to be lied to and have an election stolen from them right under their eyes."

She wasn't worried in the least. For decades the Democrats had been cheating in elections, had been selling secrets to foreign governments, - even she had made millions making shady deals with the Chinese. She knew that the American conservatives didn't have the guts to fight back. No, they would eventually shut up and back down. They always had, and they always will.

She poured herself a glass of California red wine – her favorite – and slowly sipped it. This would be the perfect coup-d'état. And, if she played it just right, she might even be able to make herself President. Oh, wouldn't that be grand?

43

The machines were running smoothly. They appeared to be flawless in how they performed the process of accepting votes, counting, tabulating, and then reporting the results. All across American the electronic machines were being set up and prepared for the next day's in-person election. All that was needed were pens and paper. At precisely eight p.m. every machine in the time zone shut down for fifteen minutes. None of the poll workers thought much about it. Most of them figured it was just preparing for the next day. What they did not know was that each machine was receiving a program update. The update would take ten to fifteen minutes to install and would become active upon a system reboot.

The small program would change two parameters of the counting procedure. The first was to count each vote for the President at a rate of .75% value, while counting those of his opponent at a 1.25% value. These numbers were chosen specifically for the purpose of hiding the impact. While the total number of votes cast would remain true, the value assigned to each candidate would be shifted. Under normal circumstances this would most likely be miniscule in its effects. However, when dealing with hundreds of thousands of votes, this simple change would alter the result by at least fifty thousand in favor of the Democrat nominee.

The second change the small update initiated was to install a new algorithm. This algorithm would keep track of the data and modify the numbers if necessary. This part of the update would only execute if the desired ratio of votes was not achieved. In essence, this meant that if, by midnight on election day, the candidate the program was intended to favor did not have a lead, the machines would automatically shut down. Upon re-booting the program would run during the start-up process and switch the appropriate number of votes to ensure the software's chosen candidate would have a lead.

When the voting machines restarted that evening there was no evidence that anything associated with the software had changed. In fact, unless someone was paying extremely close attention there would be no way of knowing the updates effected the vote counts. All that anyone would see is that the totals had changed overnight. This could be easily explained by claiming that either mail-in or absentee ballots were responsible for the difference.

44

Phillip sat down at the table with two of his friends to watch the election returns. As they had for over fifty years, the diner stayed open until midnight every time there was a Presidential election. This year would be no different. The place was packed with over one hundred patrons. Every employee was working – and quite hard. Most people had come to watch the President get re-elected. They all knew that the media had been trying to sway voters towards the opposition candidate. However, as was the case all across America, too many people had better lives now than they did four years ago.

America was back! People had more pride in the nation, better paying jobs, the President had built more wall than they thought possible, had even beaten China in a trade war – despite the fake pandemic that Ron and most of his friends saw as nothing more than another way for the elites in Washington to try and steal the election.

No, too many times he had seen tens of thousands of people at rallies supporting the President. Heck, the old, fading politician the Democrats had selected couldn't even draw one hundred to a rally. And even when he did his speeches sounded more like that of a half-baked idiot than someone who was capable of leading the free world.

Phillip looked around and saw the confidence on everyone's face. He was certain this would be a literal land-slide for the President.

45

T he news anchor looked at the results with an eye of caution. The early returns had dramatically favored the President. So much so that the bean counters downstairs had just sent a memo to the desk that there was a ninety-eight percent chance that the President would be re-elected. So confident were the decision desk members at the results that they were prepared to officially call the election for the President.

The anchor picked up his phone and dialed the number for the downstairs desk.

"Hello, can you put Bill on the line?"

"Yes, one moment."

He heard the young lady call out for Bill informing him that he had a call from the "people upstairs."

"Yes, this is Bill."

"Hey, this is Paul. I have been looking at the returns. Is there any way you are wrong? I mean, you can't seriously be expecting the President to win over 380 electoral votes? Or that he will garner more than ten million more votes than the other guy"

"Well, to be honest, those are the numbers we have come up with. I would say it is about a ninety-nine percent chance."

"Fine, but all our polls show that he should be losing – by a lot!"

"Right. Remember though, even our own polls were heavily biased towards liberals. Even the final poll only called five percent conservatives, and that poll still had the President at 43 percent."

"Serious? A biased poll calling over ninety percent liberals still had the President that high?"

"Yup. What can I say? The guy's message resonates with people. I mean, he has done nearly everything he said he would and has survived nearly four years of false allegations and attacks."

"Damn. So, realistically, what are the chances he loses?"

"Honestly? It would take a literal miracle. We would have to find over a hundred thousand votes in every single swing state to even have a chance. And I mean a hundred thousand for our guy and zero for him. That just isn't going to happen. At the current rate and projections, the absolute worst the President will do is 389 electoral college votes."

"Alright, thanks."

As Bill disconnected the call, he swore out loud.

"Shit, this is complete crap."

"What?" asked the overweight woman sitting next to him. She had been his co-anchor for nearly three years and still couldn't grasp what she was really supposed to be doing.

"Nothing. It looks like this fascist in the White House is going to win again. How the hell did that happen?"

"Who knows. I mean, Americans are a bunch of racist morons."

"Yeah, right. But every poll had him losing, and losing big!"

"Well, maybe you should pray for a miracle."

The co-anchor laughed, stood up, and walked over to the table.

Bill sat for a moment. "Well," he thought to himself, "if these numbers are correct, then it *will* take a miracle."

46

500 Griswold St, Detroit, MI. 1:00 am EST.

T he news came in fast. Voter counts across the nation were behaving in a manner consistent with what every news media and pollster had expected. It was even worse than 2016, when the President shocked not only America, but the world. For weeks it was believed that the President would lose by a margin of three to five percent. What was actually happening was that the President was winning by a significantly higher amount. In most states the count was favoring the President by over ten percent. This was not only unexpected; it was an overwhelming amount. There was no way that the plans made could compensate for this amount of difference.

Three stories below the ground level of the Guardian Building in Detroit, Michigan, there exists an entire sublevel full of offices and computers connected to a litany of servers around the nation. Every voting machine used in nearly thirty states could be accessed by the console in room B-35. In this room there were three mainframe computers tasked with tallying votes and then sending those results back to local offices across the United States. The issue these programs were running into was to massive vote discrepancy in favor of the

President. It was simply too much for the computers to adjust for in such a short amount of time.

"What do we do?" the young technician asked the dark-haired man.

"I am not sure. If we don't do something soon the system might crash and then all the votes we have switched will revert back. We can't have that. It would literally give the President the lead in over ten states where he is currently believed to be losing."

"Wow. Who knew he would get this many?"

"I don't think anyone would have guessed this."

The two men sat stunned. There was no plan for this event and they were uncertain of what to do. All of sudden the phone on the desk chirped.

"Um, hello?"

"Shut it down," said the voice on the line.

"I'm sorry, who is this?" asked the technician.

"It doesn't matter who I am. You need to shut it down RIGHT NOW!"

"Yes, sir"

The young man moved his mouse and hovered over a red "X" on his screen. He wondered what would happen if he clicked on the icon.

"Well, here goes nothing," he said.

"Yeah, better make sure they can't trace it back to you buddy," said the other man with a half-way laugh.

"Shit, I never thought of that!"

With one small motion the young man clicked the icon. For about ten seconds it seemed as if nothing happened. Then a message appeared in a small box located in the top right-hand corner of his screen: "Please confirm: shut down of servers?"

He clicked "Yes" and waited.

"Confirmed."

At that moment, in ten of the largest American cities, every electronic voting machine shut down. There was no reason given, the machines simply stopped tallying votes and shut down. At this point in time the President held a commanding lead of over one hundred-thousand votes in each of the states where the voting machines had shut down. This amounted to an Electoral College lead of 410 to 128. In the popular vote he held an astounding lead of seventy-two million to sixty-one million. Since most Americans had gone to sleep expecting to wake up to the news that the President had been re-elected in a land-slide, there were few who were aware that this event had taken place. That would change in the morning, but for now, the American election for President had simply stopped. For the first time in the nation's history a national election was put on hold.

47

T he cargo van pulled up to the back doors of the convention center. It's two rear doors opened and a man started handing large trash boxes to a worker waiting outside. In all over one-hundred boxes were taken inside. Each box held between one thousand and one thousand five-hundred blank mail-in ballots. When the ballots were taken inside, they were laid out across twenty tables. At each table there were two poll workers – all Democrats – with pens. As the van pulled away, it passed over fifteen other vehicles. Several cars, with their trunks open, also had workers carrying bags into the building. As was the case with the contents of the van, the contents of the other vehicles were brought in and emptied out on tables.

Once each bag had been emptied one of the supervisors spoke into his megaphone.

"Ok people. This is where we win. We need at least one-hundred thirty-thousand. Let's get started."

"A young college student raised her hand.

"Yes?"

"Do we fill out the entire ballot?"

"No. We don't have time for that. Only fill out the top part. For President. Leave the rest blank."

"Won't that seem odd?" another worker asked.

"No. Don't worry. Nobody is going to inspect these. We will be done before anyone else comes back. Let's just get going. The faster we can get this done, the better off we will be."

With that, every worker, at every table, began to open up the ballots and mark the vote for President. Each ballot was being cast for the President's opponent. By the time they were finished, they had marked exactly one-hundred thirty-eight thousand, five hundred and sixty-nine ballots. Every single one for the Democrat nominee. When the voting machines came back on at four-thirty these ballots were run through the system. This ballot dump caused the President's led to vanish and become a forty-seven thousand vote deficit.

Mike Shelter had woken up in a fit. His knees were flaring up again and the pain had woken him from a deep sleep. He knew he would not be able to go back to sleep any time soon, so he decided to go for a walk. He lived only a mile from the convention center and enjoyed the quiet of the early morning. With nobody out it should be a nice time to just think and let his body recover. As he turned the corner of the Detroit Riverwalk and headed toward Steve Yzerman drive, he noticed several vehicles parked outside the back of the convention center. This was odd, he thought. He had never seen any cars out this early. Certainly not parked at the rear entrance.

As he walked closer, he noticed several people carrying bags and boxes into the building. It seemed almost surreal to him. Why would so many people be carrying what looked like trash bags full of papers into the convention center? Maybe there was some kind of recycling event being set up. He thought his friends would enjoy a meme of recycling thieves, so he quickly snapped a few pictures on his phone and continued his early morning walk.

This same occurrence took place in several major US cities. Madison, Wisconsin. Philadelphia. Pittsburgh. Atlanta, Georgia. Las Vegas, Nevada. Phoenix, Arizona. Santa Fe, New Mexico. While the numbers were all different, as was the method, in each of these cities the voting machines had shut down for no apparent reason. At each location dozens of containers – trash bags, trash cans, boxes, even shopping carts – were brought in. Each filled with blank mail-in ballots. In each case these ballots were all dumped on tables where poll workers feverously filled in only the race for President. And in each city, between midnight and four-thirty am, the President's lead inexplicably vanished.

By the time the American people began waking up, the vote tally in nearly every state had changed. It seemed as if a literal miracle had taken place. For some unknown reason there were hundreds of thousands of mail-in ballots which, it appeared, had failed to be counted. At six am EST the election for the President of the United States had taken a hard-left turn. Now, it seemed, the President was losing in both the Electoral College and the popular vote.

What was a landslide victory for the sitting President had, overnight, turned into a clear victory for his opponent.

48

Phillip Stone woke up early. He turned on the television expecting to hear news of the President's landslide victory. What he heard instead confused him. During the night, it seemed, several major US cities had found hundreds of thousands of mail-in votes. And over ninety-eight percent were cast for the Democrat nominee. That seemed odd to him. How could that many ballots be missed? And once the polls closed, were they supposed to still accept ballots? He picked up the phone and called his friend Tom.

"Hey Tom, you see this?"

"Um, seen what?"

"The election results."

"Yeah man, I bet the President crushed them. He was destroying them when I went to bed last night."

"No, man. He is losing big time."

"What? How is he losing? He was up in most states by hundreds of thousands of votes."

"I don't know. Evidently, they forgot to count mail-in ballots. Or maybe they found a bunch that had been misplaced."

"You mean to tell me that the President was ahead and overnight, all of a sudden, his lead disappears because someone "found" a bunch of ballots?"

"Yeah, that's what it looks like."

Phillip thought it strange that so many votes could be misplaced. He also thought it odd that this only happened in major cities which were traditionally Democrat strong holds. While he wasn't a genius, he was also smart enough to see when something wasn't right.

49

S hawn Reynolds had just finished a lecture on the statistical theory of probability and how to formulate the chances of an event occurring. He was returning to his office when a student walked up to him.

"Dr. Reynolds! Did you see the news? The President lost the election!"

"Um, no, Sally, I haven't. I thought he was ahead last night?"

"Yeah, well, I guess he was. But this morning they found, like, a bazillion votes that were cast against him. Isn't that crazy?"

"Yes, it does seem a little crazy."

"Oh, well, what are the chances? Speaking of chances, any chance you could extend the due date on our term paper?"

"Ha. No. I am quite certain that probability is at zero."

"Oh well, you never know until you ask."

"True. Well, have a good day Sally. I'll see you

Thursday."

"You to Dr. Reynolds."

Shawn watched as the young first year grad student sauntered away. He opened up the door to his office and opened up his laptop. He did a quick internet search of the current vote status. Next, he pulled up reports from election night which also showed the vote tallies for that day.

"Hmm," he thought out loud. "That seems off quite a bit."

Shawn compared the vote counts at midnight of election day with the counts reported at six am the next day. He noticed what seemed like an anomaly. In every swing state the President was in the lead by well over a hundred thousand votes – several hundred thousand in Pennsylvania, Michigan, and Wisconsin – yet when the votes were reported the following morning his lead had vanished. The President's opponent had seemingly secured the exact number of votes needed to take the lead in each of the states. Upon reading several articles, Shawn was led to believe that this count change was due to mail-in and absentee ballots.

Shawn decided to seek the input of a colleague of his who specialized in statistical theory and probability. Shawn was well versed in statistics; however, his specialty was economics and its related mathematical theories, not statistics. He walked down the hall to the office of Dr. Ahmed Al Bibi and knocked on the open door.

"Ah, Shawn, my friend! Come in, come in."

"Good morning Ahmed. How are you?"

"Good. How are you?"

"I am well. I wanted to get your opinion on some numbers. I thought you could help me with the probability of numerical changes in this years' Presidential election. Do you have time?"

"Ah, yes. I always have time for colleagues. What are you looking at specifically?"

"Well, I am curious as to the probability of large numbers of votes going to one candidate in what seems to be overwhelming numbers."

"Ok. Well, let's look at them. Do you have the numbers, or shall we look them up?"

"I printed out the numbers from the night of the election and the next morning. I think we can start there."

"Yes, that sounds good. Let's have a look."

For the next two hours the men poured over not only the printed-out results, but results reported by several news agencies. To be as unbiased as possible, they chose to look at what are considered both Liberal and Conservative news sites. They also looked at three neutral sites which claimed to support neither candidate. What they found concerned both men. Even though Dr. Al Bibi was a supporter the opposition candidate he believed that what made America unique was that there were fair and free elections. Having grown up under the tyranny of Saddam Hussein, he knew how dangerous rigged elections could be. He wanted his man to win, but he wanted him to win fairly, not like this.

"So, Ahmed, what do you think?"

"Well, Shawn, at first glance it seems to be legitimate. When you look at each state individually, they are within the possibilities, although each one is way out on the edge of possibilities. However, when you look at the collectively, and here is where I see a significant problem, there is literally no statistical possibility that in *every single state* the former Vice-President needed to win he came up with the exact number and that each time it fell exactly within the outlying realm of probability."

"I see. That *does* seem odd."

"Well, let me explain it like this: You flip a coin ten times. You get seven heads and three tails. Seems odd, but, okay, it is possible. I mean, there is only a seventeen percent chance of that actually happening, but it is possible. Now, if that was the only time it happened you would not be too worried. Now, let's say you flipped the coin in ten flip segments. Now, you do this eight times and each time you get seven heads and three tails. This is impossible. This is, essentially, what took place in the election."

"So, it would appear that a serious statistical anomaly occurred?"

"No. what I am telling you is that a statistical impossibility occurred. There is no possible way that the election results would see that much change in favor of one candidate. Even considering that mail-in ballots favor the Democrat candidate, it is still a statistical impossibility that the difference in votes would be so consistent across every single state."

"I see. So, how would you go about actually proving this?"

"It is actually pretty simple. All you need to do is look at the numbers. You take the totals reported at midnight on November 3, and then the numbers reported the following morning. Compare and do the math. That will give you the information you are looking for."

"Ok. Now, what would you say if I told you that in every one of those states the counting process was stopped late that night and was not continued until early the next morning?"

"I would say that someone had planned this."

"And what would the probability be of this happening in several states?"

"Again, that would be odd for one or two states. It would be impossible for this to occur in several states. Again, consider the coin-toss scenario. Temporarily stopping counting in one or two states is odd, but would not be out of the realm of possibility. However, stopping the counting in five or six states is extremely odd. Stopping them only in states that a candidate was losing but needed to win – all on the same night, at the same relative time, with the same exact results of the President's opponent taking the lead? Impossible. You would have a better chance of flipping a coin ten-thousand times and coming up heads every time."

"Great. Now. How do we prove this? And, how do we get this to the people who can actually do something about it?"

"Ah, my friend. These are questions I cannot answer. I am just a simple professor who likes to be in his class discussing theory with students. I know little of the things you ask."

"Thank you, Ahmed. I truly appreciate your help. Do you mind if I take all of these papers with me?"

"Of course not. Perhaps there is a Doctoral Dissertation somewhere in here for pone of our students?"

"Perhaps. That, I think, is a question for another time. Good day my friend."

As Shawn left his friend's office and walked down the hall, he could not help but think about who could possibly have the ability to commit such massive fraud. Not only that, but who could do this with seemingly no evidence left behind?

50

As the election results continued to pour in several of the major news networks began to call the election for the Democrat nominee. According to nearly every political pundit, the President had lost the election due to the massive numbers of mail-in ballots. In nearly every swing state these ballots went against the President by a count of nearly eighty to twenty percent. In several major cities the numbers were even more dramatic. Cities such as Philadelphia saw a vote tally rate amongst the mail-in ballots favoring the former Vice-President by a ninety-two to eight percent difference. To most observers this would seem nearly impossible. However, the media claimed that the President's supporters had, for the most part, voted in person, whereas the Democrat supporters had chosen mail-in due to the national epidemic.

As the President sat in the Oval Office watching the latest news coverage, he became increasingly agitated. He had been warning the American people of how easy it would be to commit fraud with mail-in ballots, but even he was not expecting it to be so wide-spread and on such a massive scale.

"This is...pretty bad. How are they so sure they

will get away with this?"

The Presidents' Chief of Staff responded.

"Well, sir, they have the media, big tech, and numerous governors and judges on their side. I know you have been warning them for the past three years, but it appears that they just don't care."

"No, the American people care, they just don't know. We need to make sure that they know. I want all the evidence we can gather put together and given to our legal team. This just cannot be left alone. This country cannot become a socialist oligarchy, not on my watch."

"Yes, Mr. President."

As the room cleared, the President asked one of his most trusted legal advisors, a former mayor of New York City, to wait behind. He wanted a few moments of privacy with him.

"Listen, we need someone on the outside, who doesn't work for us directly, to do some digging. Someone who is tough and will not quit. You know anyone?"

"Yes, sir, I do. I can get in touch with her and see if she is game."

"Are you certain she is up to it?"

"I can guarantee you she is. She is one of the toughest federal prosecutors I have ever dealt with. She doesn't quit. And she doesn't do anything without proof. We can be assured that if she makes a claim, she can back it up a thousand percent."

"Good. Get in touch with her. She can't officially

be part of the team because that could compromise her efforts if she is receiving White House funding."

"Got it. Give me a few days."

"No. Get it done today. We can't wait."

51

The former Federal Prosecutor sat in her home office watching the news. She was aware of the possibility of voter fraud – especially with all of the mail-in ballots. She was also acutely aware that in the majority of sates absentee and mail-in ballots could only be sent to those who first requested them. According to most state laws, any votes which are solicited are not eligible to be counted. This would mean that an estimated six million votes were illegally cast in the 2020 election. All she needed was time and proof. She had never moved forward with a case without rock solid evidence. The question was whether or not the President's team would even consider her.

The phone on her desk rang twice before she picked it up. She did not recognize the number and was not expecting a call.

"Hello?"

The conversation lasted only five minutes, but it would have major consequences for both herself and the American people. She had been asked by the lead lawyer from the President's legal team to help them. She understood that she would not technically be a part of the team, nor could she rely upon any funding from either the White House or the President's national party organization.

She was fine with that. She had amassed enough savings and investments to last her several years and realized that there were certain avenues of investigation she could not follow if she was a part of his team. No, she was prepared, had the time, and knew exactly where to start.

Today was going to be just grand for the former prosecutor. And tomorrow would begin the fight of her life.

52

Phillip sat at the counter in his favorite restaurant and smiled as Selma poured him his third cup of coffee.

"Thank you, Selma."

"You are welcome, Mr. Stone."

"Please, call me Phillip. Mr. Stone is my father. Gosh! Please tell me I don't look like a seventy-five-year-old!"

"No, sir. You do not look that old."

"Good."

He switched his attention to the television hanging in the corner.

"Nice tv there," he thought to himself.

The tv was tuned to one of the major news networks. The show was covering the recent legal suits filed by the President. According to the anchor the President was refusing to accept defeat, even though every major news organization – liberal and conservative alike – had declared his opponent the victor.

"And today we hear of yet another law suit filed, this time in Georgia, claiming that hundreds of thousands of illegal ballots were cast. This is the fourth state where the President's legal team is trying to overturn the election. It appears that even now he is plotting to steal the election."

Philip literally laughed out loud. For four years the same station had refused to accept the President's victory in 2016, claiming that the Russians had somehow committed vast fraud in an effort to elect the current resident of the White House. That conspiracy had been so thoroughly debunked and proven false that even the current Speak of the House, one of the most ardent opponents of the President, had stopped mentioning Russia. It seemed, however, that the major news media had forgotten this.

"Well, Selma, what do you think about the election? Kind of a mess, isn't it?"

"Well, even with all that is going on, America is still the best country in the world. Where I came from it was pretty bad."

Selma had never spoken to anyone in the town about her past. She was afraid of how they would look at her if they knew she had been used to carry drugs illegally over the Mexican-American border. And she wanted to forget as much as possible all of the physical and mental abuse she had endured. She remembered that it was only when the abuse turned sexual that she had found the courage to fight back. Oddly enough, her assailants attempt to kill her is what ended up saving her life.

She wondered what the old Park Ranger that found her was up to and if she could ever really thank him.

"Were elections this bad where you came from?"

"No. They were actually worse. I can remember that no matter how many people voted the same people seemed to always win. Whoever had the backing of the local cartel would win. Even when it was clear that one person had overwhelming support, it seemed that the vote counts always changed by the time the official count was made. I think that his election in America today reminds me of that."

"Really, how so?"

"Well, for one, I don't know anyone who voted for the President's opponent, do you?"

"No, I actually don't. At least not around here."

"Second, the other night when we were watching the results come in, the President was so far ahead it seemed nearly impossible that he could lose. Then when we wake up the next morning, all of a sudden there were millions of votes around the country which were 'found' by his opposition. And they all literally were against the President. This is exactly what would happen in my old home."

"Yeah, I thought that was kind of odd myself. How would so many votes just randomly show up at one time? And all of them, or at least the vast majority anyway, be cast against the President? Seems shady to me."

"Well, if you ask me, I would guess America had a cartel trying to steal the election. But nobody asked me, so...."

"Well, I asked you," Phillip said with a laugh.

Selma returned the laugh, "Yes, you did."

53

Cambridge, Massachusetts, the corner of Broadway and Ellery Streets, June 3rd, 1976, 2 o'clock a.m.

T he young man was stunned. The lady had come from nowhere it seemed, and had just appeared in his headlights. There had been no time to react. He simply could not stop the car from performing its deadly act. He knew it was hopeless when he stepped out of the vehicle and ran around the back. He saw the shape of the body on the road – motionless and silent. Slowly he approached her and bent low to see if she was breathing. All he could hear was a low, guttural sound. He saw a dark liquid dripping from the corner of her mouth. He smelled alcohol on her and noticed a needle and a bag of powdery substance had fallen from her purse when she hit the ground.

"Good," he said to the night, "if she is a druggy then nobody will even be looking for her."

He checked her purse to see if there was any identification. Nothing. While it was terrible that she had stepped out on front of him, at least she was nobody who would be missed. He began to relax and tried to assure himself that everything would be okay. He just had to move. He had worked too hard, too long, to escape the steel mill. For years he had studied harder than anyone he knew. First in the small Catholic school, then as an undergraduate student. When he was admitted to Law School then made editor-in-chief of the Law Review paper he knew he was on his way. But this! This would change everything. He had been at a party celebrating the graduate students who had just matriculated and earned their Jurisprudence Degrees. He could just smell the alcohol on his breath and knew that, regardless of what actually happened, he would be in deep, deep trouble should a police officer happen by.

As the young man thought for a moment about what to do, he saw the bright lights of a car out of the corner of his eye. He froze, thinking that someone had driven up on the scene and would see him. His heart skipped a beat when he realized it was just a reflection on one of the nearby windows from a townhome across the street. He quickly walked back to his car, closed the door, and quietly whispered "I am sorry." He did not look back as he drove away. Nor did he ever speak of the incident to anyone over the next forty plus years.

429 Broadway Street, Cambridge, Massachusetts, June 3rd, 1976, 2 o'clock a.m.

The man was awake, mostly because he had just finished writing a letter he hoped he would never send. He had been tasked with finding young lawyers and recruiting them to the cause. It had proven more difficult than he had expected. These Americans were brash and arrogant. Even the youth were reckless – concerned with only what they could gain. And the college youth were the worst. He had tried sublet suggestions of wealth and power, but the students remained aloof to him. It seemed they all wanted success now and were unwilling to wait. He turned off his desk lamp and stretched.

He heard the tires shriek outside his second story window. He quickly crossed the room and peered out onto Broadway Street. There, in the middle of the road he saw a man stooping over a body – presumably a female based upon the way she was dressed. He silently watched as the man checked the pulse, quickly looked around and ran back to his car. As the car sped away, the man noted the make and model of the car. As luck would have it, he light from the corner lamp reflected just enough for his to read the last four digits of the license plate.

As the car turned left on to Trowbridge Street, the man in the office picked up his phone and dialed the number on his card.

"I think we have someone."

"Good. Can we use him?"

"No, not now. But perhaps we can groom him."

"Good. See to it. Remember, time is an ally. Do not be hasty."

"I will not."

Rafael Abdullah Aphasia hung up the phone and thought to himself, "Time is an ally."

The incident was filed deep in the mind of Rafael. He knew that time would indeed return his reward with patience. He did not know that it would be over forty years before time would repay him.

54

Office of the Chief Justice of the United States
Supreme Court, December 8ᵗʰ, 2020.

As the Chief Justice of the United States Supreme Court, the man was the highest-ranking jurist in the country – if not the world. He had been appointed several years ago and had remained fairly quiet, with the exception of siding with the liberal justices when it came to health care and Second Amendment Rights. He was not concerned about the election, as he believed the states would work out the issues.

He began his day as every other, coffee and toast with a reading of the early edition of a few of the national papers. He liked having them in print – his eye sight was starting to bother him and his pride refused to allow him to wear glasses in public, so he would spend an hour every morning reading print papers.

His most recent clerk came through the door and handed him a manilla envelope.

"Chief Justice, this just arrived from the mail room for you. I had it checked by security because there is no return address."

"Thank you, Charles. I'll get to it after my papers."

"Yes, sir. Is there anything you need? I was going to go over the next three oral arguments and type up background briefs for you."

"Hmm...that would be great. Please be sure to notate specific precedence for each? If you can find three or four cases for them, that would be sufficient."

"Yes, sir. I will see what I can do."

"Good. I'll be in chambers for most of today. The Justices will not be meeting until tomorrow. I think the new Justice is getting a tour of the building."

The Chief Justice placed the manilla envelope on his desk and spent the next half-hour reading through two major newspapers. When he finished the second one, he took off his glasses, rubbed his eyes, and let out a long exhale. He was still young for a Chief Justice, but he could feel age sneaking up on him. He thought back to his college days and how much energy he used to have.

"Well," he thought to himself, "time is no ally to the old."

He picked up the manilla envelope, opened it up, and pulled out two pieces of paper. The first was a typewritten note on heavy letterhead. On it was one sentence:

HAVE YOU FORGOTTEN THAT NIGHT?

The second piece was an eight by ten photograph. It was obviously an old picture – black and white – but there was no doubt as to what it showed. There, lying in front of the Chief Justice of the United States Supreme Court, was a picture of him looking directly at the cam-

era. It was late at night and he was kneeling over the body
of a young woman who had been hit by a car.

The Chief Justice froze. His heart began racing and
he broke out in a cold sweat. He had almost forgotten
about that night so long ago. His life had gone forward
exactly as he had planned. He had been sure that nobody knew about the accident. Yet here on his desk was
a picture which would implicate him in the death of this
young woman. He looked back at the letter and noticed
the telephone number in small print at the bottom of the
page. He could not afford for this to become public as it
would ruin his career.

The Chief Justice picked up his phone and dialed
his secretary.

"Yolanda, I need to step out for a while. I am going
to head over to the archives and do so research on a few
cases coming up. Please take any messages for me."

"Yes, sir. Do you know when you might be back?
You have a meeting with the President's Chief of Staff at
two-thirty."

"I should be back before then."

He hung up the phone and walked to the side entrance. As he stepped outside the building, he used his
personal cell phone to dial the number.

"Hello?" said a deep voice.

"Hello. To whom am I speaking?"

"Oh, I do not think that matters, does it, Mr. Chief
Justice?"

"Yes, it does matter. I don't think you understand

who you are dealing with."

"Yes, I understand completely. I understand I am dealing with a scared man who is responsible for the death of a Senators daughter."

The Chief Justice froze. A Senator's daughter? He remembered reading about the sad death of a Senator's family member in a driving accident around the same time as.... well, this. He had never put the story together though. It made sense now. The woman he had hit had been drinking and looked like a prostitute. That was one of the reasons he thought nobody would pay attention. It was just another street walker involved in a random accident. Obviously, the power holders in Washington could not afford the negative press of America finding out one of her most trusted Senators had a daughter who was a drug addicted prostitute. It had probably been easy to concoct the story – especially in the late seventies when there was no internet and no cell phones.

"So, Mr. Chief Justice, perhaps you would be willing to discuss a way we can both make this go away?"

"Go on," he said.

"I will send one more letter within the week. On it will be a fairly simple request. If you follow it, this picture disappears and will never be seen again."

"And if I refuse?"

"I think you know what would happen then. We will not require you to break any laws or commit any overtly unethical acts."

"I see. And how do I know I can trust you?"

"Mr. Chief Justice, I have had this picture for over forty years and no other person has ever seen it. Trust me, if I want it to go away, it will go away."

The line went dead.

55

Article III Section 2 of the United States Constitution States:

"THE JUDICIAL POWER SHALL EXTEND TO ALL CASES, IN LAW AND EQUITY, ARISING UNDER THIS CONSTITUTION, THE LAWS OF THE UNITED STATES, AND TREATIES MADE, OR WHICH SHALL BE MADE, UNDER THEIR AUTHORITY;-TO ALL CASES AFFECTING AMBASSADORS, OTHER PUBLIC MINISTERS AND CONSULS;-TO ALL CASES OF ADMIRALTY AND MARITIME JURISDICTION;-TO CONTROVERSIES TO WHICH THE UNITED STATES SHALL BE A PARTY;-TO CONTROVERSIES BETWEEN TWO OR MORE STATES;-BETWEEN A STATE AND CITIZENS OF ANOTHER STATE;-BETWEEN CITIZENS OF DIFFERENT STATES;-BETWEEN CITIZENS OF THE SAME STATE CLAIMING LANDS UNDER GRANTS OF DIFFERENT STATES, AND BETWEEN A STATE, OR THE CITIZENS THEREOF, AND FOREIGN STATES, CITIZENS OR SUBJECTS.

IN ALL CASES AFFECTING AMBASSADORS, OTHER PUBLIC MINISTERS AND CONSULS, AND THOSE IN WHICH A STATE SHALL BE PARTY, THE SUPREME COURT SHALL HAVE ORIGINAL JURISDICTION. IN ALL THE OTHER CASES BEFORE MENTIONED, THE SUPREME COURT SHALL HAVE APPELLATE JURISDICTION, BOTH AS TO LAW AND FACT, WITH SUCH EXCEPTIONS, AND UNDER SUCH REGULATIONS AS THE CONGRESS SHALL MAKE."

It was the second clause that concerned the Texas Attorney General. He had been paying close attention to the current slew of court cases being brought by allies of the President and he thought most of them were either based upon opinion or lacked strong legal backing. He knew the current court make-up would probably favor the President; however, he also knew that the court was not favorable to involving itself in political struggles.

Well, at least most of the court. The current Chief Justice seemed to be turning into a social justice warrior.

The Attorney General had been a Constitutional lawyer prior to his election. He had served as a clerk for the late Supreme Court Justice Antonin Scalia and had learned from him to have a deep abiding faith in the United States Constitution. Not only that, he had also learned that in order to maintain the Republic – for the United States was a *republic*, not a democracy as most people believed – the best way to interpret the founding document was through the lens of a strict constructionist. Essentially this means that if the Constitution does not expressly grant the government a power, it does not have it. This also meant to the Attorney General that those powers given to the government at inviolable.

He sat down and called in his assistant, a newly graduated lawyer from the University of Texas.

"Pam, can you do some research for me?"

"Yes, sir."

"Good. First, check US election law. I want to know if there are any Supreme Court case which have granted states wide leeway in choosing electors. Second, find out of there are any laws or precedents where either executive or judicial branches of state governments can effectively ignore their own state constitutions and statutory laws when it comes to the election process. What we are looking for should apply to federal offices. I don't think we would have standing when it comes to state or local elections."

"Got it. Anything else?"

"Yes. I need this ASAP. Whatever you have slated for today just got bumped. Take any of the clerks you think you will need. And Pam, if you need all of them, take them. We are in a severe time crunch here."

"Yes, sir."

The Attorney General flipped through his phones book and selected the names and numbers of several Constitutional lawyers who had argued before the Supreme Court in the past. He also decided to give a call to this own Senator. He was perhaps the best Supreme Court litigator he knew and wanted to get his opinion on his idea.

After putting together his list he decided to do a little research himself. He had been able to rely upon assistants and clerks for decades and had forgotten how much he enjoyed this aspect of his job. And with the internet it made it so much easier than the old card catalogs and massive indexes he used when he was in college.

It did not take long for him to find what he was looking for. It was a short law passed in 1845 in response to the Presidential election of 1844. In that election James K. Polk, the Democrat nominee, was running against Henry Clay, a Whig. While Polk won the election and there were no questions of his legitimacy, the election itself continued for over a month. The first votes were cast on November 1st and the last votes were accepted on December 4th.

In order to prevent future elections from taking so long to determine the winner, the twenty-eighth Congress of the United States passed a relatively short law called "An Act to establish a uniform time for holding elections for electors of President and Vice President in all the States of the Union." The law states – in simple terms – that the states must have selected their electors for President and Vice President no later than the date of the election. In essence, Federal Law does not allow for any votes to be counted after the date of the election.

The Attorney General wanted to check one other thing – had the law ever been amended or changed? He could find several laws which slightly altered the election process, yet every law passed reaffirmed that all electors must be chosen by the end of election day. He also realized that, since this was a federal law, state governments could not change it. This meant that any law passed by a state legislature, any decree by a governor, or any decision by a state court, which allowed electors to be chosen after the date of the election would be unconstitutional.

He realized that his state had followed the law as written. Other states had not. His own state had gone as far as refusing to count any vote not received by the date of the election. This was sound legal doctrine and had not been challenged by either political party in his state. His next thought was that, since his state had followed the law and others had not, there was an imbalance.

If voters in other states had been allowed to have their votes counted after the election, then this amounted to an unfair election. Since the election for President and Vice President were federal in nature, then the Voting Rights Act of 1965 was applicable. And this meant that every vote for President must be treated equally. If the state of Texas followed federal law while other states did not, this would mean that those states who counted votes after the day of the election had violated the Voting Rights Act and had disenfranchised millions of voters around the country.

He decided at this point to draft a writ to the Supreme Court. While he understood the importance of voting and voting rights, he also believed in the law. And the law must be followed. He also knew that this issue could not wait to go through the federal court system. Since Article II of the Constitution gave the Supreme Court of the United States original jurisdiction in cases between states, he believed he could go directly to the Court if he filed a case on behalf of the state of Texas against those states which had allowed post-election day voting.

It did not take long for him to put together the document. He only needed to make sure the language was based upon sound legal arguments and that there were no precedents which would negate his argument.

Seven hours later a messenger arrived at the North Drive on Second Street in Washington, D.C. Here he hand-delivered the document prepared by the Texas Attorney General to the clerk of the United States Supreme Court. Once the clerk had notated the reception of the document, he sent it to the Justice who was "next-in-line" for receiving cases. Within fifteen minutes the Justice requested that the entire court meet in the conference room.

The decision was ultimately procedural in nature and was essentially a formality. The court decided to accept the briefs of not only Texas, but also several other states which had decided to file *Amicus Briefs*. The Chief Justice also decided to expedite the case because of its implication on the Presidential election. He decided to give each side twenty-four hours to prepare. The justices all agreed that they would reconvene in two days to go over the original suit and the accompanying briefs.

56

When the Chief Justice returned to his office, he found another manilla envelope on his desk. He asked his secretary to hold all calls and closed his door. He dreaded what he knew was in the envelope, yet he had to open it and read it to be sure. On a single sheet of stationary, he read the note:

YOU CANNOT ALLOW THE COURT TO HEAR ANY CASES ASSOCIATED WITH THE CURRENT ELECTION FOR YOUR PRESIDENT.

His hands were shaking. He knew that he could not stop the justices from meeting and at least discussing the case. While he could not stop the court from considering the challenge, he also knew they had not formally decided to hear arguments. He had one chance. He could convince the eight other Justices that the court did not belong in the political realm. He had to. His entire career and life were at stake and he would not sacrifice it all because of a drunk harlot.

57

The conference room of the United States Supreme Court is a long and narrow room decorated with wood paneling and soft oriental carpeting. Sound is dulled by the hundreds of volumes of legal decisions. There is a black fireplace at the South end which provides more of an aesthetic appeal than actual heat. Unknown to most Americans is that the room also serves as a safe room in the event of a terrorist attack on the capitol. The room can be sealed off and provided with an independent air system. Due to these changes made in response to the September 11th attacks in 2001, the room is virtually sound proof.

The Justices sat and discussed the recent case filed by the Texas Attorney General. All nine were present and deeply concerned about the entire situation.

The newest member – only recently appointed – was paying close attention to the others and taking notes. She wanted to get an idea of how each presented their opinion before she offered hers. She had learned that, as is often the case, how one made an argument was as often as not just as important as the argument itself.

The Chief Justice was speaking to the constitutionality of the case.

"While the Voting Rights Act does allow for litigation when disenfranchisement occurs, I am not certain that it meets the smell test. While Texas may claim that its citizens have been treated unfairly, it is, again, the role of the state legislatures to create and enforce voting laws, not this court."

"Perhaps," said the courts lone black jurist, "but the Constitution is expressly clear that when any state files a suit against another, this court, and no other, has original jurisdiction. Whether the case itself has merit, and I believe it does, it cannot be heard by any other court. I do not see the harm in at least hearing oral arguments."

The room was silent for a few moments. The Chief Justice was not used to being so openly challenged, especially by this justice, who rarely spoke during oral arguments or during conference sessions.

"Well, the issue is not whether we have jurisdiction, it is whether the case itself has merit. If we see no pathway to a positive ruling for the state of Texas, I fail to understand why we would even entertain the case. It is not the job of this court to determine the winner of a Presidential election, nor to impose our will upon the American people."

The newest court member spoke in a soft, but clear, tone:

"Perhaps we are looking at it incorrectly? Texas argues that, since the selection of electors for President and Vice-President are federal in nature, even though the methods of selection are left to the states, then the Voting Rights Act does come into play. Since every vote cast in a Presidential election is essentially equal, is it not the job of this court to assure that every vote, regardless of which state they were cast in, is equal?"

"Again," said the Chief Justice, "the Constitution is clear – states do, in fact, have the right to alter election laws within their boundaries as long as every voter in that state is treated equally. The Voting Rights Act was not intended to be a catch all to be spread across every individual state. Even though Texas may have one set of voting statutes, it does not mean that every state must have identical ones."

The conversation continued for several hours as each justice made their case for or against the filing. In order for the case to be heard, it would take four of the nine justices to vote to accept the case. The current make-up of the court was conservative, six to three, however the Chief Justice routinely sided with the court's liberal jurists. It was a foregone conclusion that the court would agree to hear the Texas case, and, when the vote was taken, the result was just that - five to four in favor of hearing arguments.

As the Chief Justice gathered his papers and headed back to his office, he began to consider how to convince just one of the conservative justices to his side. He knew that the most likely choices were the two newest members and he was hoping both would agree with him. He only needed one, however a six-three vote would be more acceptable than a five-four vote.

He sat at his desk and thought about how to approach the topic. When he made up his mind, he summoned his secretary.

"Yolanda, would you ask the two newest members to meet me in my chambers? Thank, you."

58

Roger Caldwell sat at his desk overlooking the city of Chicago. He loved the city, it was perhaps the only thing in his life he truly did love, and he had purchased the building solely for the view his current office gave. He could look out over both the city and lake Michigan. It was located on the corner of West Adams Street and South Franklin Street. The height of the building dwarfed every nearby structure except that damned Sears Tower. He thought that was the uncomeliest building in the city. A tall, blocky, black structure that looked like it rose straight form the depths of hell, he thought. It just didn't fit in with the Chicago school of architecture.

As he gazed out at Lake Michigan his personal desk phone chirped.

"Hello," he sighed.

"Yes, Mr. Caldwell, this is Stephen."

"Yes, Stephen, I know it is you. I am not a complete fool you know."

"Um, yes, sir. I was calling to let you now that the Supreme Court agreed to hear the Texas case. It had been docketed for three days from now."

"I see. Well, I wouldn't be overly concerned with its Stephen. I am fairly certain the Chief Justice will vote in our favor."

"True, but with the new member, we still are one vote short. Would you like Rafael to make a visit?"

"No, leave him out of this. He has done enough with the Chief Justice. I think we can use our tech friends to pressure the court. While they claim they are immune to public opinion, we both know that none of the justices want to look bad in the press. Well, except the one from Georgia."

"Ok. I will give them a call."

Roger set the receiver down and ended the call. How ironic, he thought. The state of Georgia was the one place where his people had made the most mistakes and here it seemed that the most powerful conservative voice on the court, who was the one person in America most likely to dis-rail his plan, just happened to be from the same state.

Well, he had dealt with previous justices who tended to get in his way. He remembered the last time an ultra-conservative justice refused to bend to his will. All it took was a ten-thousand-dollar payment and a pillow. It was sad, when he thought about it, how little the doctor asked for to simply change his official findings from homicide to natural causes. How anyone could believe that man could die from a heart attack due to sleeping with a pillow over his face was beyond him. Yet, that was what the official report suggested.

This time he wouldn't go to such drastic measures, but he had convinced one jurist to retire when her husband had become suddenly, and most severely, ill. That was even easier.

People were fools, Roger thought to himself. They would believe whatever a person in authority told them, no matter what the evidence said. He was banking on this one last time.

59

The red-faced man pressed the end icon on his phone and called in his vice-chair.

"Hamad, do you have few minutes?"

"Yeah, what's up?"

"Listen, we need to step up our defense of the election. I can't just stand by and do nothing while the President tries to overturn the will of the American people."

"I hear that! That fool just can't take no for an answer."

"Well, it seems like the Supreme Court is on his side now, too. This must have been why he was so adamant to push through his nomination so quickly. He knew he was going to lose and made sure his minions on the court would be in his back pocket."

"True. He has a six-three majority, doesn't he? Kind of sucks, man."

"No. I think the Chief Justice will side with truth. He may be a conservative but he isn't a fanatic like the President. No, I am more concerned with the two newest members. They are unknowns."

"So, what can we do about it? Those old cronies probably don't even have a cell phone!"

Both men laughed at that statement.

"Well, you know I hate to censor speech. My entire purpose for founding this company was to give the American people, and the world, a platform for the free expression of ideas and thought."

"I know. But sometimes we have to point out the lies that the right pushes on people. I agree, free speech is important, but lies and misleading content can't be allowed to go unchecked."

"Right. Listen, just this once, I think, in order to make sure we save the country from that orange buffoon, we may need to go a little bit further than before."

"Hey, man, I am with you. Hurting a couple of neo-Nazi judges in order to prevent a coup is a no-brainer."

"Good, I am glad you agree. Let's step up our disclaimers and post blocking. I want every post dealing with election fraud taken down. Also, I hate to do it, but, increase account bans to a minimum of four weeks for anyone who spreads stories about election fraud."

"I'm on it."

"Thanks."

After Hymned left his office he dialed a number from memory. It was the third time he had placed the call in just over six months. He did not like speaking to the man on the other end, he seemed strange, but he also realized that it was not him he was really working for.

He was happy to help the committee. After all, it was Mr. Caldwell who had really funded his company years ago, and without that help he would have never been able to grow into the world's largest on-line meeting place.

"Hello?"

"Mr. Hammonds?"

"Yes. How are you?"

"Fine, thank you. I was just calling to let Mr. Caldwell know that we have dome what you asked. The restriction will be imposed for four weeks. Any longer and it might draw too much attention."

"I will let him know."

60

CNN Headquarters, 1 CNN Center, Atlanta, Georgia

The President of the nation's largest cable news agency sat alone in his office. He had just spoken with Stephen Hammonds and was irate at the news that the Supreme Court was going to help the President steal the 2020 election. He was so mad, in fact, that he had one of his famous tantrums.

When he finished his litany of curses and throwing two coffee mugs against the Plexiglass windows, he calmed down and summoned the head of the domestic news services.

"Listen, John, we need to do something, something big."

"Yeah, what is that?"

"The Supreme Court is going to hear a case which could overthrow the election and give it to that dumbass in the White House. I need everyone on board. We have to stop this, and I mean like yesterday!"

"Whoa...calm down man. We got this."

"Fine. I just hate that man. He has tried to destroy

us since day one. Listen, I want everyone you have on this. Dig up everything you can on the two newest Supreme Court justices. Hell, make stuff up, I don't care. And bring back that stupid blonde woman. Maybe we can use her again."

"Right. You know she failed miserably last time? Hell, she was such an obvious fake half the Democrats didn't believe her. But, man, if you want to."

"Do it. I want it ten times a day and all over the internet. Saturate them. And come up with something about his new one. Maybe make up some crap about her kids, how she mentally abuses them or something. Just cite anonymous sources. That always works."

"Okay, man. Whatever you want. How deep do you want to go?"

"Listen, freedom of speech is on the line. We can't sit by any longer and allow this man to take us back to the dark ages. Go as deep as you can. I don't care how bad it is. Once he is out of office we won't have to worry about any blowback. That idiot who is replacing him doesn't even know what office he was elected for, so..."

"Gotcha. You want this out today or tomorrow?"

"Start it on-line as soon as you can. Then have some stories ready for prime time. Once they release, we can just watch it roll."

"Roll man, roll! We got this. It's payback time, man. Payback."

61

T he pressure placed upon the Supreme Court, along-
side the arguments of the Chief Justice, tipped the
balance in favor of the President-Elect. When the decision of the court was made public, it caused a firestorm
among the nation's news agencies.

The decision was highly ambiguous and full of
legal jargon most Americans could not understand. It
took a local news anchor to sum it up in a way that most
people would be able know what the ruling actually said.

"Well, it looks like that's the end of the President's
bid to overturn the election. The Supreme Court today
ruled against the state of Texas."

"Well, Pam, they actually ruled for Texas, but
against the President. The court essentially ruled that, in
terms of the law, Texas was correct in citing violations
of the Voting Rights Act. However, the court also stated
that Texas' case was not made in good faith and that it
was, in and of itself, an attempt to disenfranchise millions of voters."

"So, basically what you are saying is that Texas
won *and* lost?"

"It looks that way, doesn't it? The court made it clear that, since the state only filed the case after it was apparent that the President lost, there was no true attempt by the party in question to request a statutory review, but, rather, it was, and I quote here, "a last-ditch effort by the President to negate the results of the popular vote" end quote. What is interesting is that the court also decided that, in order to prevent this type of confusion in the future all electors must be chosen on election day."

"Really? That's interesting."

"Yes. It seems there is a little-known law from 1845 that required all electors to be chosen on election day. The court said that, since traditionally states have counted ballots after election day, they will allow this years' contest to include them, but that in the future they will not count."

"Well, better get up early next time. Now, onto weather. Ben, what can you tell us about this winter storm heading our way?"

62

She had never seen her husband this angry. In all the years they had been together she had seen his temper only once. He had suffered losses that most people could not fathom. His wealth had nearly been wiped out in the eighties and even then, he was not this angry.

"What the hell were they thinking? No good cause? What better cause is there than the United States? These people are literally nutts."

"Sir, we can still try to reach out to the state legislatures. They do have the authority to select their own electors."

"No, Mark, I won't go that far. We did everything right. We proved fraud, proved it beyond a doubt! And now this? What the hell is going on around here?"

"It goes too deep sir. When the swamp has its tentacles in even the Supreme Court, well...I don't know."

"Neither do I. I never realized how deep it went. Good lord, man, does anyone in this town care about the American people and the law?"

"It is like you said, they care about how the people

can give them more wealth and power."

The Vice-President spoke up.

"What do you want to do?"

"Let me think about it for a minute."

The room was silent for nearly ten minutes as the President thought about what the best course of action would be.

"Okay. Here is what I want. We can't go against the Supreme Court, not if we truly believe in the rule of law. Even though they are full of it, they are the final say. Mark, get the President-Elect on the line. John, prepare a statement for release. No, wait, I'll give it in the Press Room. I want everyone there. And I want all the fraud evidence on a table in the room. We may have lost this fight, but the war is not over. Not by a long shot."

63

Pitcairn, Colorado

P hilip Stone watched the press conference in silence, just like everyone else in the diner. It was packed to beyond occupancy. It seemed like every time there was some type of major news the little diner on main street would be full of members from all across the county. He noticed Selma standing in the kitchen doorway, her eyes filling with tears.

"Hey, Selma, are you okay?"

"Oh, yes. I think so. I just do not understand why he has given up. He is such a string leader and to just quit...I do not understand."

"I don't think he has given up the battle yet Selma. It is like I learned in the Army. Sometimes you have to retreat in order to regroup and come back stronger. I think this is what he is doing. He can't fight the Supreme Court and all the states at the same time. That would be suicide. Maybe, I hope, he is making what we call a tactical retreat in order to come up with a stronger plan of attack."

"I hope you are right. I have seen so many men in

my home town who just could not stand up to the evil and they either quit or were silenced. I hope the President knows what he is doing."

"I believe he does. He fought hard and, like most of us, proved that the swamp was deep and would do anything to stay alive. Even steal an election. It is obvious we can't save America through the courts, maybe not even through elections. But we are a nation of laws and the President, more than any may I know, respects the law. No, I am sure he hasn't given up."

Philip wrapped his arms around Selma and held her tight. He had grown to care about her over the past year and did not like the fear he saw in her eyes. It had been several years since he had cared like this for a woman. When his wife died from cancer five years ago, he had focused on his kids and trying to help them over come a life without a mother.

Maybe, he thought. Maybe the future will change for America. And, as he looked down into the deep brown eyes of Selma, he thought maybe, just maybe, the future will change for me.

64

Roger Caldwell sighed. A deep, relaxing sigh. They had won. *He* had won. His last-minute campaign against the two justice's morality had succeeded. Nobody, it seemed, even the innocent, can withstand the scrutiny and pressure of an entire world. He knew there was more work to be done. He wasn't so sure that the President-Elect was as cognitively aware as his advisors claimed. He had known the man years ago in law school and even then, he seemed a simpleton.

Now it was time to step back and relax, if only for a moment. He could let the wheels of power in Washington run freely for some time. It would only take the usual amount of grease to keep it going, and he had plenty of that. Even the so-called Republicans in Congress could be bought. After all, he had made sure none of them would stand behind the President. Only two members actually backed the President all the way. That pesky member from Ohio's 4th district was too law-and-order to be bought and the upstart from California's 22nd was just as bad. Even worse, he thought. After all, he had nearly the entire state of California on his payroll. Who would have thought that a member from the nation's most liberal state would be such a staunch supporter of the nation's most conservative President?

Oh well, he thought, there are only two of them. He can let them have there moments and sound bites. They could not do any damage now that the election was officially over.

Stephen Hammonds entered the room through the side office door.

"Mr. Caldwell, the committee is waiting."

"They can wait a little longer Stephen. I have waited several decades."

"Yes, sir."

As Stephen left the room Roger looked out over the city he loved and a smile came to his face.

He spoke out loud even though the room was empty.

"Ah, Chicago! You tried me with that Muslim man. I knew he would fail. His arrogance would never let him be controlled. But here we are. We have the one who I can bend to my will. And bend her I will."

65

*Wednesday, January 20th, 2021. East Portico
of the US Capitol Building*

I t was a cold crisp day in the nation's capital. A slight wind was blowing in from the Atlantic. The sky was clear with the exception of a few small clouds left over from the previous night's storms. Attendance was high and the people were spread out all along the lawn from 3rd street to 14th street. They ranged from Constitution Avenue to Independence Avenue. Not since the first inauguration of FDR had so many people been in attendance. They had come to see the man they thought would change the world for them. And, indeed, they did see that man. He just wasn't the one taking the oath.

The President-Elect placed his hand on the Bible held by the Chief Justice of the United States Supreme Court. He repeated every word the justice uttered in a clear and loud voice.

> "I do solemnly swear that I will faithfully execute the office of president of the united states, and will to the best of my ability, preserve, protect and defend the constitution of the united states."

A thunderous applause ripped through the city.

Echoing down the mall and bouncing off the Lincoln Memorial. The cheers made their way across the Potomac River and faded away as it passed over the former home of Robert E. Lee. It was as if the sound refused to awaken the thousands of souls buries deep within the former Confederate General's estate.

As the newly sworn in President gave his inauguration speech, he seemed to fumble with the words a few times, catching himself once form going off target. He had been told to stick to the script and speak slow enough so that he did not get the words mixed up. He made it through the twenty-five-minute speech with relative ease, only having mixed his words twice. No matter, his wife thought, he had a grueling campaign and an even worse time waiting for the election to finally be over. And besides, the media loved him. Surely none of the reporters present today would mention it.

Roger Caldwell sat six rows behind the President. He had attended every inauguration since Dwight Eisenhower's second one. While a man of his wealth and power could command a seat much closer, he had never been one to let pride get in his way. Let them have their moment, he thought about all the men and women who were sitting closer. He understood who had the real power in Washington. He could walk down the street alone and nobody would even notice him. Just an old man, maybe a retired Congressman or some lobbyist. Most people saw the tall, thin man, as just another face in the crowd and he preferred it that way. He did not need the attention of men to feed his pride. H had far more important things to concern himself with. One of them sat in the first row next to the former Vice-President.

66

T hree weeks into the new administration, the President's Doctor was called to the second floor of the White House. This is where the President and his family live during his time in office. The doctor made his way down the center hall, through the doorway leading into the West Sitting Hall and turned left to enter the Master Bedroom of the White House. The President was lying in bed covered, his wife sitting beside him. In the room was the President's Chief of staff, as well as his son.

"What seems to be the problem?" he asked the First Lady.

"I am not sure. He came down with a fever late last night. I put him to bed and gave him some ibuprofen for his temperature, but it hasn't gone down."

"Okay. Well, lets see what we have."

The doctor took the President's temperature. He furrowed his brow when he saw the number. One hundred seven. Not good. He immediately called the Walter Reed emergency room and notified them that he was bringing the President in for observation overnight. His temperature was dangerously high and he seemed confused as to where he was.

The White House staff sprang into action as documents were place in briefcases and items from the Oval Office were marked and placed into several boxes that would accompany the President to Ward 71, the place where the President receives medical care which cannot be given at the White House. The trip is usually a short ride in Marine One from the South Lawn to Bethesda. The helicopter lands directly on the hospital grounds and the President is escorted by Secret Service agents into the building.

This trip was no different than any other taken by the past seven Presidents who had an overnight stay. As Marine One landed at Walter Reed Medical Center, the President's staff was crossing into Maryland on Wisconsin Avenue. It would take them longer to arrive, although at this hour it would be a fairly short ride.

Several tests were given to the President over the next twelve hours in an attempt to discover what was causing his illness. The medical staff had been able to lower his temperature to just under one-hundred, but this required a constant supply of ibuprofen. They were not too concerned about the medicine, rather they were concerned about the cause. He had tested negative for almost all know viruses and was not displaying any symptoms associated with anything other than the flu. And yet, he did not test positive for the flu. At around nine a.m. the final test result came back. The President had contracted the Novel Coronavirus.

When the President's Doctor gave the news to his wife, she received it stoically.

"Ironic," she said. "He has done everything right and still he gets it."

"Well, madam First Lady," the doctor replied, "there is really no foolproof way to prevent one from contracting the disease. Contrary to what you may believe, cloth masks are not capable of stopping the spread."

"I thought they could? That is what all his advisors told him."

"Well, ma'am, I hate to be the one to tell you this, but in my thirty years of serving our national leaders, I can assure you that your so-called advisors are going to tell you what you want to hear, not the truth."

"How do you think he will do?"

"I really don't foresee any problems. He is rather old but other than that he seems to be in good health. I suggest we keep him here for at least a week, or until he presents no more symptoms."

"Ok. I will let him know when he wakes up."

Unfortunately for the First Lady, the President never woke up. He passed away two days later at two-thirty a.m. As the President's doctors worked feverishly to save him a dark-skinned elderly man made his way to the second-floor elevator. No one noticed the small syringe he tossed into the waste basket, nor the nod he gave to the nightly charge nurse. There would be no investigation into the President's death, as it was determined that he had succumbed to the coronavirus. And there would be no need for the nurse to explain how she could now afford four years of college for her twin daughters.

67

The Vice President took the oath of office in the second-floor conference room of her residence located at Number One Observatory Circle, US Naval Observatory, Washington, DC. She was literally shaking, never having considered that she would be taking the oath of office as the forty-seventh President of the United States.

The people gathered in the room included her husband, step-children, parents, and sister. Also present were her chief of staff, personal assistant, two Secret Service agents and the Chief Justice of the United States, who, for the second time in two months, had to preside over an oath of office.

68

Chicago, Illinois

Stephen Hammond dreaded his next task. Roger Caldwell was a patient man, but even he had his limits. And to be so close once again would probably drive the old man to his grave. Nonetheless, he had a job to do.

"Sir, do you have a moment?"

"Yes Stephen, I have several moments. Come in."

"Sir, I have some rather bad news."

"Well, before we discuss this sudden terror you seem to be bringing me, let's sit for a drink, shall we?"

"Um, sir? I don't think this is a good time for a drink."

"Nonsense. I always have a drink when I find success. Do you not celebrate your own victories?"

"Well, yes, sir. But we have just been dealt a serious blow to our plans. Mr. Caldwell, I came to inform you that the President has died and the Vice-President took the oath of office twenty minutes ago."

"Yes, Stephen, I know. That is why we are celebrating."

"I don't understand."

"No, I suppose you would not. Did you really think this was all about an old man who couldn't even remember his wife's name? No, son, we needed youth in the office. That was the plan all along. And now we have her right where we want her."

Stephen sat in silence, stunned at the news he was just given.

EPILOGUE

R odney Stillwell had worked as a janitor for over thirty years in TFC Center. He was nearing retirement and was looking forward to a quiet life with his wife and eleven grandchildren. He had lived in Detroit his entire life and had only left for four years during a stint with the US Navy. He was nearing the end of his late-night shift and had just completed cleaning the second-floor restrooms. He rolled his cleaning cart into the storage room and, when he turned to hit the light-switch he kicked a small object across the floor. Bending over, he discovered a red piece of plastic, no larger than his thumb, lying on the ground.

"Ha," he said out loud. "I guess that is why they call them thumb drives.

Rodney was my no means a tech savvy man, but he had paid attention when his eldest grandson explained to him all the new gadgets the kids seemed to love nowadays. He placed the drive in his pocket, tuned off the light, and closed the door.

"Three weeks, Jerry." he said to the other night shift janitor.

"Yeah Rodney, three weeks and you get to fade into obscurity."

"Man, I would be happy to fade away. Just me, Bernice, and the grandkids. What a life that would be. 'Course those young ones might be a little rowdy now and then, but I do love my babies!"

"Well, I am happy for you Rodney. If anyone had earned the right to a quiet retirement, it is definitely you man."

As Rodney slid into his 1965 Ford pickup, he could not have known how the information on that little drive would change not only his life, but the life of the entire nation.